Drawing with Light

JULIA GREEN

Bloomsbury Publishing, London, Berlin, New York and Sydney

First published in Great Britain in March 2010 by
Bloomsbury Publishing Plc,
50 Bedford Square, London, WC1B 3DP

This edition published in May 2012

A CIP catalogue record for this book is available
from the British Library

ISBN 978 1 4088 1957 9

MIX
Paper from
responsible sources
FSC® C018072

Printed in Great Britain by Clays Ltd, St Ives Plc, Bungay, Suffolk

1 3 5 7 9 10 8 6 4 2

www.bloomsbury.com
www.julia-green.co.uk

For Rosemary

Notebook 1
September to December

1

'Where are you? Kat? Emily?'

'Em-il-y?' Cassy's voice echoes round the still, hot garden.

I'm wriggling up, about to call back, but a hand grabs my arm.

'Shh!' My sister Kat pulls me down lower, under the tall grass and flowering plants and fruit bushes where we are hiding at the bottom of the garden.

Lying on the hot ground so close, I can hear her heart thumping as if it is my own. The air is heavy and sweet with the smell of hot grass roots and the tang of blackcurrants: above us the ripe fruits hang in shiny black clusters along the branches. Too sour to eat raw: we tried earlier and had to spit them out. In any case my tummy is full to hurting with the raspberries and redcurrants we've been stuffing into our mouths all morning.

'Ow. You're squashing me.'

'Shh, you great goon. Shut up or she'll find us!' my sister hisses into my ear. She's pressing me down so hard my face is rubbed into the hard edge of the book she was reading to me. I try to lift myself up enough to

1

tug it out from under me but she's pinning me down too tight, as if she wants to be mean and hurt me. She'll swear she didn't, when I say, later.

Why doesn't she want Cassy to find us? Cassy has come to look after us. Cassy is soft and kind and when she reads stories she doesn't hiss or frighten me like Kat does. But Cassy *is not our mother, Kat says, and we must not like her. And then she might go away.*

When Kat says the words 'our mother', my head goes fuzzy. The stories make me scared but I have to keep listening anyway; it's like I can't stop.

When Kat is at school, sometimes I get the book out of the blue drawer where Kat keeps it. There's one picture about halfway through the book of a pretty lady with dark hair and a blue silky dress who is drinking water from a stream under some trees. I say the fuzzy words 'my mother'.

Cassy has stopped calling. She's gone back into the house.

'Sit up, then, silly,' Kat says. 'Look what you've done to the book! It's all squashed.'

'You made me. You did it on purpose.' I start to cry.

'Stop that right now, crybaby,' Kat says. 'I didn't do anything to you. I'm reading you stories, aren't I? So listen.' She starts over again, reading aloud our favourite story.

I lie down on my back so I can see the blackcurrants shining in the sun and the way the light makes patterns through the grasses when they move. I suck my thumb even though 'you're too big for that now you're four', Dad says. I twist the hem of my dress in my

2

other hand, round and round. My favourite blue dress, all soft and comfy except it's getting tight under my arms now and today it has red stains all down the front, from the berries.

'At the edge of a big forest there lived a poor wood-cutter with his wife and his two children . . .'

Kat does her telling-a-story voice, which makes me sleepy, to begin with, until the horrid things start to happen. In the story, I mean. Not for real, though sometimes I get them mixed up.

My earliest memory. It's the first memory I have of something connected to my mother. So perhaps that is the right way to begin to tell this story.

2

Bit by bit, I'm writing down what happened, those months we lived in the caravan, Cassy and Dad and me. Kat was away, mostly, at university, but she is part of the story too. Kat was there from the beginning, of course.

I want to include other things: fragments of memory, scraps from the past which help me make sense of it all. It's like making a patchwork quilt, sewing together the pieces of my life, stitching in the squares and making something whole. I could add the photos: I've got more than enough of those now. The letters and emails too. And a painting.

Perhaps it's more like a scrapbook than a quilt, then. In any case, it helps, writing this down. But where to begin is hard. There's the memory, which is the earliest moment. Or there's September, and my first meeting with Seb. If it hadn't been for Seb, I'd never have arrived at where I am, now. Meeting him made it all possible.

You open up your heart and then things happen you couldn't imagine, before.

So here's another starting point: an evening, in September.

It's dusk.

Kat and me are picking our way over piles of stone and rubbish, into the middle of the big downstairs room in a house more like a ruined castle than a home. Tumbled-down walls, swathed in ivy; moss like bright green pincushions on the stones. It smells of damp.

'It's a total wreck,' Kat says. 'Dad's really bonkers this time. He might as well build a new house from scratch.'

I lean against the thick stone wall that divides the downstairs space. At the top, where the stone has crumbled, an ash sapling has taken root and sent thin pale shoots up towards the light coming through a hole in the roof. Ferns are growing out of the same ledge, filtering the shafts of grey light.

I can hear the river even from inside. It sweeps past the house in a big curve below the mound the house was built on centuries ago, almost a moat. It's easy to imagine ghosts: the people who lived here, over the years. Voices half caught, echoing off stone.

When it's all restored, Kat and me will have rooms right at the top, under the slope of the roof. Dad's shown us his plans, drawn with his neat architect's pen, black ink on thick white paper. We'll have our own bathroom and sitting room, even: just the two of us. Dad and Cassy's room will be on the first floor, with two spare bedrooms. The downstairs will be a huge kitchen and living room, and two studies: one each for Dad and Cassy. It's hard to imagine, though. Kat's right. It is a wreck. A ruin on a grassy mound in the middle of a field, miles from anywhere.

'Is it haunted, do you think?' I say.

'Don't be daft,' Kat says. "Course not. You don't still believe that rubbish, do you?' She starts poking around the smaller room at the back, peering up the fireplace – what's left of it.

I wander back to the doorway. The sun's gone right down since we first arrived, on bikes, but even so, it's lighter outside than in the house.

Someone's opening the gate. It clicks shut behind him. My heart starts to thud. He crosses the field, towards the steps up to the house. He hasn't seen me: I suppose I'm hidden in the shadow of the doorway, and he obviously isn't expecting anyone to be here.

If I'd been alone, I might have thought of ghosts, to begin with. He's wearing some sort of black jacket. His hair's shoulder-length, dark. His collar's turned up, and his hands are in his pockets. I can see he's real, now, as he comes closer: dark jeans, bright green trainers, nothing like a ghost from the past, but a really beautiful boy with fine features, a slim build, dark eyes.

He's only just noticed me.

He stops, halfway up the steps. 'Oh.' He looks embarrassed.

'Who's that?' Kat comes up behind me. 'What's he doing here?'

The boy half smiles.

I can feel the change in Kat immediately. She sort of melts and softens. 'Hello,' she says.

I turn round to look at her.

She's smiling. With one hand she twists her hair back from her face and over one shoulder, like rope.

'My dad's going to be working here,' the boy says. 'He said about the house . . . I came to look. I didn't think anyone would be here, this time of day.'

Kat steps forward, pushing past me. 'It's our house,' she says. 'I'm Kat and this is Emily.' She waits.

The boy looks uncomfortable. So she prompts him. 'And you are?'

'Oh. Seb.' He does that half-smile again.

'Hello, Seb,' Kat says. 'We can show you round, if you want?'

Of course he wants. Kat has this way of making people fall in love with her, just like that. It's partly the way she looks: long golden hair, pretty, slim, smiley – all the usual things. But it's also the way she takes charge: people love that. I've seen it loads of times.

He follows her round the house, while she points out its features – stone mullioned windows, huge chimneys, massive oak beams, stone roof tiles. I suppose what with his dad being a builder he might be interested in that stuff. Most people his age wouldn't be. He's about seventeen, eighteen, I guess.

I watch them: he's dark, Kat so fair and golden. They look good together. He has this faintly amused look on his face while Kat chatters on, slightly mocking. Every so often he turns round and smiles at me.

I seem to be unable to speak a word.

'And while it's all being restored to glory,' Kat says, 'I shall be happily far away at university.' She gives a little triumphant grin. 'While Dad, Cassy and Em have to rough it in the caravan for the winter!'

Seb looks at me again. 'Here?' he says. 'In a caravan?'

'No, on a site with loos and showers, a mile away,' Kat says. 'Luckily. It's too awful, living on a building site. Dad found this cute caravan on eBay. It's proper seventies style, like the real thing, not retro.' She goes on and on, practically explaining our entire life history, about moving around because of Dad being an architect and all that.

I can see the boy's getting edgy.

Kat's looking a bit manic. 'This is Dad's dream house. It will be, anyway, when it's all finished. Six months. Do you think they can finish it in six months? Dad says that, but he's always wrong. He's always way too optimistic about how long things take for real.'

'There's going to be six stonemasons, I think, working full-time,' the boy – Seb – says. He talks quite slowly, as if he is thinking carefully about what to say. 'So they might manage it.'

'What do *you* do?' Kat turns the beam of her full attention on him.

He looks awkward. 'Not much. This and that. Odd jobs that come up.'

His voice sends prickles up and down my skin, like goosebumps.

The three of us walk to the door. It's totally dark now. There's no electricity of course, no street lights or any house lights for miles. The river sounds louder in the dark.

'How did you get here?' Kat asks him.

'I ran. It's what I do – running, I mean.'

'We've got our bikes,' she says. 'But we could all walk back together, if you want.'

'It's OK,' he says.

He's clearly itching to get away. I imagine he'd wanted to wander around by himself, not be given her guided tour and running commentary. Still, he can come again, another time, can't he?

'I wasn't really trespassing,' he says, going down the steps. 'Sorry.'

'It's, like, totally fine,' Kat says. 'Any time! Not that I'll be here. I'm off to York tomorrow.'

We watch him go. The darkness swallows him up.

Kat gives a big sigh.

'What?' I say.

'He's gorgeous! Isn't he?'

'Yes.'

'Typical. Just when I'm leaving home, the most good-looking guy in the world shows up.'

'You'll be back at Christmas,' I say.

'Suppose.'

'And there will be millions of good-looking blokes at university, won't there?'

'Yes. And he's a bit young, and he doesn't have a

9

proper job. So he's not The One.'

We pull the door closed. It's so ancient and rotten it doesn't lock. We get our bikes from the side of the house.

'Did you bring lights?'

'No.'

'Me neither.'

'It's not far. It won't matter.'

A strange thing happens to me that night, cycling in the total dark. I keep thinking I'm going to bump into a wall or a tree or something. The dark is so thick it seems solid, a physical thing. It's as if all my other senses have gone too, along with my sense of sight. I wobble and fall off a million times and Kat gets the giggles. But after a while she realises I'm serious: I really can't see where I'm going, and I can't balance, either. We end up walking side by side, pushing the bikes.

'If we hurry,' she says, 'we might catch up with Seb.'

But we don't. There's no sign of him the whole length of the lane. We could just as well have dreamt him up: the product of our own imaginations. Or was he a ghost, after all?

We turn left on to the main road for a short distance, then left again down the narrow tree-lined lane to the camping field. In the far corner, the white caravan glows in the dark, all lit up within. Dad and Cassy must be back with the takeaway. It's our last night with Kat. She's going on the train to York in the morning, and I won't see her for eleven weeks. It's the longest we've ever been apart.

At bedtime, I'm still thinking about the boy. Seb.

His dark hair, and his olive skin, and his brown eyes. And the way my heart beat faster, and my skin started to dance, little shivers running up and down my spine.

3

Right now I'm typing with my laptop on my knees, perched on the seat that runs along one end of the caravan. Dad and Cassy aren't home from work yet, which makes it easier to get on without interruptions, questions, Dad looking over my shoulder with suggestions for improvements (spelling, grammar, style). I've just pulled the curtains at all the windows. When the lights are on, the caravan's a bit like a ship lit up in a sea of dark, and I start imagining someone watching me, seeing I'm here by myself. From the inside, looking out, I can't see a thing, so I wouldn't be able to tell if someone was out there or not, would I?

I'm missing Kat.

She left on 29th September, which is exactly one month ago.

The clocks went back at the weekend. It was already beginning to get dark when I was walking back from the bus stop after school this afternoon. I have to walk by myself, of course; no one else at school lives way out in the middle of nowhere like this. And no one else has a dad mean or crazy enough to make them live for six months cramped up in a tiny caravan in the middle of a field while he works on renovating a house.

An ordinary newish caravan with a proper toilet and shower would be bad enough, but this is beyond a joke. Like Kat said, he found it on eBay: a bargain. Orange decor. Plastic table. Baby Belling cooker with two electric rings. No running hot water. A chemical loo that stinks, so we have to use the site toilet – and shower block – instead, which means going outside. The living room is tiny: if I hold out my arms I can almost touch both walls. Dad and Cassy have to sleep on the pulled-out sofa seat because there's only one bedroom, with bunk beds. Dad thinks it's fun, like being on holiday, but that's because most of the time he isn't here. He's at work, in a warm office, or doing site visits or whatever.

Even with my feet hunched up under my big woolly jumper I'm still cold. Back in sunny September, the caravan was too hot all the time. Now it's freezing. We're the only caravan left on the site.

I switch on the kettle, make tea so I can warm my hands up on the mug. I ought to be doing homework. I've got loads. I'm doing three subjects for AS level: Photography, English, Geography. I check emails: nothing from Kat. I check her out on Facebook and find a load of new photos: Kat at parties, mostly, looking slightly drunk and happy, with her arms round different people. Friends I don't know.

It's pressing on my mind, what happened in the Photography lesson today. Something my teacher said . . .

13

I start off by doing the actual homework, which is researching a famous landscape photographer: Ansel Adams. Millions of sites come up. I make some notes in my photography journal:

1902–1984
California; B & W photographs; landscapes (wilderness)
Realistic approach: sharp focus; heightened contrast; precise exposure.

And then I type my own name in, the way you do: searching out different identities, the other Emily Woodmans I might have been. The zoologist Emily Woodman, or the one who won a sailing regatta, or the daughter of some peer ... and then I look at Emily Carr, because she's one of the famous Emilys I'm named after, along with Emily Brontë (novelist) and Emily Dickinson (poet). According to Kat, it was my mother's idea. My real mother, that is: *Francesca,* not Cassy.

Cassy's our stepmother, but we don't call her that because it makes her sound wicked, like in stories, and she's not at all. She came to look after us when I was about four and Kat was six. She married Dad when I was seven. She's much younger than Dad; people sometimes thinks she's our big sister, even though she's got wild, wavy red hair and pale skin with freckles and doesn't look anything like either of us. Kat's hair is long, golden and gorgeous; mine is short, dark and spiky. When I was little I wanted it long like Kat, but Dad said it took too much time in the morning, what with all the combing and plaiting for school.

I scroll down the screen, to check out the postage-stamp-size photos of paintings by Emily Carr (1871–1945). I start clicking on the images to enlarge them. Fir trees. A log cabin. Totem poles. A child sitting on her mother's lap. I love her paintings of trees. My favourites are *Above the Trees* and *The Little Pine*: young trees full of light and happiness against a darker background of mysterious forest that looks as if it is alive and moving.

A car bumps across the rough field. Headlights sweep across the curtains. The car brakes; doors slam; voices. They're back.

Cassy stumbles in and dumps two carrier bags on the floor. She swings her hair back, smiles. 'Em! You OK? Sorry we're so late!'

Dad flicks the kettle switch as he walks through the kitchenette. He nods at the laptop. 'Homework?'

I've logged off the website already. I feel weirdly guilty, as if he could tell what I was about to do. My next search . . .

Cassy lays out the foil dishes on the Formica table-top. 'Prawn korma, vegetable biriani, onion bhajis and rice.' She hasn't looked so happy for ages.

'What's this in aid of?' I ask.

'Nothing.'

'Just a rest from cooking,' Dad says.

I get out some cutlery; Dad opens a bottle of beer. He pours two glasses. 'Want some, Em?'

'No thanks.' I don't like beer much, and in any case, drinking with your parents just seems weird.

'So,' Dad lifts his glass. 'Here's to us, and *la dolce vita.*'

'La what?' Cassy wrinkles her nose up, which makes her look about ten.

'The sweet life. It's a film,' I explain.

Dad smiles at me above Cassy's head. He still finds it amusing, the things she doesn't know, even after all this time.

The rest of the meal, they talk about the house, and then about work, and laugh a lot. I just want it to be over. I can't work out why they are so over-the-top cheerful. Without Kat here, it's as if the balance has shifted. I'm the odd one out. They egg each other on, and think everything is funny. Even after we've cleared the table and Cassy and me are watching TV, Dad keeps looking at Cass. He's only had two beers. It's gross. I take the extension lead, so I can plug in my laptop on the bunk bed, and leave them to it.

Alone in here, lying on the bottom bunk, I pluck up my courage and try again. The internet connection is painfully slow. I type the name in a second time. Francesca Woodman. I press *Search*. But nothing comes up. Nothing relevant, I mean. No photographers, no famous artists, no one who might be my real mother.

Today is the first time I've thought about her for ages. I was two when she left; I don't even remember her face. But something Mr Ives said in Photography, earlier today, has started me off again.

16

One tiny throwaway remark.

'Wonderful work, Emily. You've got a particularly good eye for light. An artist's attention to detail.' He was leafing through my photography journal, where we stick in our most interesting photos, and write notes on the processes and stuff like that.

He turned over another couple of pages, to my sequence of black and white photos of the trees on the lane down to our field. And then he said the words.

'These are so like Francesca's work! Remarkable. It must be in the genes!'

I went cold.

Mr Ives didn't notice, of course. He was already moving on, to someone else's table, picking up another journal and leafing through.

Dad and Cassy are giggling. The walls are paper thin: I can hear everything in too much detail. I put on headphones, listen to music. I give up my search on the internet, email my friend Rachel and Kat instead. There's a message from Rachel:

come and stay over at the weekend?

yes, I type back.

At some point, the whole caravan shakes when Dad or Cass goes out for a pee, and the door bangs back on its hinges. The wind's got up. It rocks the caravan and whistles in around the loose metal window frames. I feel a second blast of cold air when the door opens again and Dad/Cassy comes back in. I check the time: 11.40.

I turn out the light, get properly undressed and

snuggle under the duvet. On this top bunk, I'm only about ten centimetres from the ceiling. It gets claustrophobic if you start thinking about it too much. I lift a corner of the curtain and stare out into the darkness. A thin crescent moon is rising: *a sky canoe.* Is that from a poem? Wordsworth? Coleridge? Cassy's voice murmurs something to Dad; I can't hear her actual words, just the low whispering. Finally it's silent, apart from the wind. Still I can't sleep. My mind is racing.

I lean over and scrabble in the box on the shelf next to Kat's bunk. I know it'll be here somewhere. My hand finds the hard edge of a book, the raised pattern of letters on the cover. I pull the curtain back further, so I can see better in the silvery moonlight.

Kat and I looked at this book so often when we were little that the pages became unstitched. On the inside front cover, a bookplate shows a lion and a unicorn holding an open book between them, and in the middle are printed the words: *This book belongs to_____.* In the space, the name *Francesca* is written in blue ink, in careful joined-up writing.

My finger traces around the letters, the loops and curls. This is our mother's book, from when she was a little girl, which she left behind with Kat all those years ago (fourteen years, nearly fifteen). The paper's soft, yellow at the edges and mottled, from damp. It's all I have of her, and so very little to go on. Over the years, even her name, *Francesca,* has become this unmentionable secret in our family.

I turn the pages. In the faint silvery light, I begin

to read the story that Kat used to read aloud to me. *At the edge of a big forest . . .*

The words are stepping stones, taking me back to the feeling of being very little, and afraid. The words are white pebbles glowing in the moonlight, showing the way back . . . and I'm not sure I want to go there, after all, or what I will find if I do.

But before I have gone very far, I'm already drifting into sleep, and dreaming . . . and it's not my mother, Francesca, who comes to me then, but Seb.

4

He's like a magnet, pulling me in.

The second time I see him, it's at the house, again. It's a Friday, so I get home early, while it's still light. I don't have any lessons Friday afternoons and you're allowed to go home to study.

I change into jeans and trainers, sling the camera in my shoulder bag and pull my bike out from under the tarpaulin behind the caravan. I have to wipe the saddle and brush the cobwebs off from under the seat. I haven't used the bike since we last went to Moat House, Kat and me, over a month ago. Kat's bike's there too, with a flat tyre.

It's uphill all the way to the main road, then along a bit on the level, and then downhill the rest of the way. Whizzing down the lane under the trees with their autumn leaves all orange and red is amazing, like travelling through a tunnel of golden light. I stop at the beech tree near the gate to take some photos: the trunk and branches are black silhouettes against a blaze of coppery leaves, the whole thing lit from behind by the sun, low in the sky.

I can't see any vans, or hear the *tap-tapping* sound

of chisels on stone: perhaps the workmen knock off early on Friday afternoons? I park the bike up against the farm gate, push through the smaller wicket gate beside it. The low sun casts long, deep shadows over the grass.

I walk slowly up the steps to the front door and push it open. All the rubble has been cleared away. The floor is just earth, but clean-swept. I can see for the first time what it might be like when it's finished: the big, airy living room with its huge fireplace, the kitchen looking out on to the river. Once the new French windows are installed it will all be flooded with light.

My eyes adjust and I freeze. Someone is here after all, with their back to me, crouched at the foot of the scaffolding. For a moment my eyes can't quite take in what – who – exactly I am seeing.

Seb turns. He looks startled too. He's holding some sort of building trowel in one hand. He scrambles up to face me. He's wearing blue overalls, like painters and decorators wear, except he's covered in stone dust.

'Hello,' he says.

'What are you doing here?'

'Repointing the stone.'

'I mean, why? Are you supposed to be doing that?'

'It's OK. Just helping my dad out. He's gone to get more sand. He'll be back in a minute.'

We stare at each other. Without Kat here, everything's completely different.

'I've got to take all the old mortar out. Very

carefully, by hand. It takes ages,' Seb says. He starts work again, raking out the loose stuff between two stones, ready for the new mortar which will stick it all back together properly, to make the wall sound and strong. He's only done about one millionth of the wall so far.

'That'll keep you busy for about a year, then,' I say.

'You *can* speak. That's four whole sentences.'

I glare at him. The cheek!

'Your sister did all the talking, when we met before,' Seb says. He does that half-smile, sort of teasing.

'Well. She likes to talk.'

'You don't?'

'Not as much as Kat. Only when I've something to say.'

'Has she gone, now? To her *university*?' The way he says it makes it sound as if he is mocking Kat. As if going to university is not something he would ever do.

'Yes. She's in York,' I say. 'Not back till December. Sorry.'

'Why sorry?'

I don't answer. I suppose I'm expecting him to be disappointed that it's me here, and not Kat. People usually like Kat more than me. Boys do, anyway.

'Have you come to take photos of the house?' Seb asks.

My hand automatically touches the camera, still round my neck. 'No.'

'What, then?'

'You are very nosy,' I say. 'I came to see how the

house . . . what was different.'

'And the camera?'

'It's what I do. Photograph things.'

'A hobby or a passion?'

He's taking the piss, presumably.

'A passion. And it's for work.'

He looks a bit impressed. 'Really?'

'Yes, A-level work.'

'Oh. That.'

'Yes.' I'm half waiting for him to make some sarky comment about school. I imagine he hasn't been for ages. But he doesn't.

We study each other. Between us, something sizzles. A kind of energy.

I'm thinking: he's so beautiful. Pity he's sarcastic. It spoils him.

He's thinking: I haven't a clue what he's thinking.

I'm slightly dizzy – from the cycling, or the sun, or being so close to Seb, I don't really know why. I might tip forward any second . . .

A large bird flies up through the gap in the roof. The flap of its wings makes us both jump back. Its mewing cry echoes round the stone shell of the house. It's an eerie, wild sound.

'A buzzard? In here?' Seb says.

'I suppose it's the perfect place. For a nest or whatever.'

'They don't nest in the autumn!' Seb says.

'Sorry to be so stupid,' I say.

'I didn't mean that . . . it's unusual, to see a buzzard in a building, that's all.'

'When will they mend the roof?' I ask.

Seb shrugs. 'More stonemasons are coming next week. That'll speed things up. It's been a bit slow so far. Just Dad and me. I should get on, really.' He turns back to raking and scratching at the stone.

I watch him.

It's very strange to think of Seb working in our house, getting to know it close-up, stone by stone.

'Can I take a photo?' I say.

'It's your house. You can do what you like.'

'No, I mean with you in it, working at the stone.'

He shrugs. 'If you want.'

But there's not enough light. I need the tripod, for a long exposure.

'Nice camera,' Seb says, stopping work again.

'Thanks.'

'Expensive.'

I flush. 'It was a birthday present.'

'When was your birthday?'

'Summer. June.'

We both step back when we hear the van engine slowing down at the gate, as if we've been standing too close and don't want anyone else to see.

I walk back to the open doorway to see who's arrived. A white van is drawing up outside the gate. A thick-set man with messy dark hair and olive skin like Seb gets out. I watch him lift my bike away from the gate, open it and drive through. He parks the van, goes round to open the back doors, starts pulling at something in there.

'Seb?' the man calls up.

I stand to one side to let Seb go through the doorway, down to help his dad.

I push the heavy wooden door closed and walk back into the middle of the house. Even with the gaps and spaces, the stone walls seem slightly warm, as if they've soaked up the day's sun and are now slowly releasing it. I keep my hand against the stone. Something in me gives, as if I've been holding on to my breath and now at last can let it go, alone in the house just for a minute or two.

I can hardly take it in, that I'm actually going to be living here. My room will be at the top, with the view over the river and the fields beyond, and all the space I could ever want. It will be worth waiting for. Six months, Dad says. Six months is bearable. Perhaps this really will be the house where Dad settles at last, and we won't ever have to move on again. We will be properly *home*. I think it's all I've ever really wanted, to feel that.

I hear footsteps on the stone steps. I turn as the front door swings wide open, spilling golden evening light over the earth floor.

'Hello there!' Seb's dad wipes his hand on his T-shirt and holds it out to shake mine. 'Rob's daughter? Pleased to meet you. I'm Nick.'

'Emily,' I say. It's funny shaking hands. His hand is warm and dry, sort of dusty. I glimpse Seb in the doorway: that half-mocking smile.

His father is big and muscly and old. But once, he would have been good-looking. He's got the same colour skin, and the dark stubble, and deep

25

brown eyes, like Seb.

'We're just about packing up for the day,' Nick says. 'We've a bag of sand to bring in, and then we'll be off home.' He moves towards the bit of wall where Seb was working, frowns slightly, and rubs at the stone with his hand.

Seb's face tightens.

'Not bad,' Nick says. 'But you need to work faster than that if you're expecting to get paid.'

Seb's about to say something, then stops himself. He looks furious.

'I'm going now too,' I say cheerfully, to break the tension between them.

Nick smiles at me. 'She's a grand house, isn't she? She's going to be, anyways. When she's had a bit of TLC. Give us a hand with the sand, then, Seb. We need to get it under cover.'

I can hear their voices rising and falling – well, Nick's, anyway – as I walk over the grass. It's damp with dew already. I push my bike to the lane. When I look back, Seb's standing at the top of the steps, watching me. I wave at him. It's a test. My challenge to him: what will he do?

He waves. Not so cool and ironic, then, that he won't do that.

I think about him as I cycle home. That sarcastic, mocking tone in his voice. It's like he's defending himself from something. It's just a mask, really. He's learned to do that. It's not the *real* Seb.

Kat will be dead jealous that I've met him again. Or maybe not, now she's in York with all her new friends.

Perhaps I won't mention it. It's not as if anything's actually happened. A bit of conversation, a *feeling* of something important, that's all.

Cassy's lying with her feet up on the sofa when I get back. 'Where've you been?' she says, in a sleepy voice that shows she doesn't really care.

'I went to see the house.'

Cassy sits up a bit. 'And?'

'That's it. Then I cycled back.'

'How is it coming along? Have they done much?'

'Hardly anything. Still that big hole in the roof, and the tree growing out of the top. There was a bird in there. A buzzard.'

Cassy sighs. She looks totally wiped out.

'Shall I make you tea?' I say.

'Would you? Thanks, Em.' She closes her eyes again. 'Are you going out, later?'

'Yes. Said I'd see Rachel. I'll need a lift, though.'

'Your dad can take you. When he's back.'

'I'll stay over. You and Dad can have the place to yourselves for a bit.'

Cassy doesn't seem to hear. I fill the kettle and switch on my laptop while I wait for the water to boil.

Kat's on MSN.

– *How's things?* she types to me.

– OK. Missing you. How's uni?

– *Awesome. Having a really good time.*

– I saw your photos on Facebook.

– *Yeah – people from my flat. I really like them.*

Anna, Ell, Maddie. Plus Simon.

   – Simon?

   – *He's in my biology seminar. Got to go now –
making supper xxx*

She's signed off before I've a chance to say anything at
all about me. Or Seb.

5

'Soon as you're seventeen we'll teach you to drive,' Dad says.

He lets me change gear on the ride over to Rachel's. I've been doing it since I was about ten. Cassy gets cross and says it isn't safe, but according to Dad I'm learning about cars that way. I had a go at actually driving, when we first came to the caravan field. I laughed so much I went round in a big circle and almost into a hedge.

'Now!' Dad says, just before the bridge.

I do a smooth gear shift down to second. 'We'll need a second car, if I'm driving too,' I say. 'And there's the lessons. I'll have to get a job.'

Dad frowns. 'Not with A levels coming up. There's nothing more important than your education, Emily. It's the passport to your future . . .'

Yes, Dad. Like you haven't said that about one million times already.

Rachel's mum's standing at the open front door when Dad pulls up outside their house. She's got a bit of a thing for Dad: she was probably waiting at the window, ready to leap up the minute she saw the car. She comes down the steps to speak to him.

'Hi, Amanda,' I say as I climb out. 'You look nice.'

She flushes. 'Thanks, Emily.'

She's wearing new jeans and a rather nice blue wrap top. I think of Cassy, slumped on the sofa in her woolly jumper and sloppy old trousers. Dad probably doesn't even notice.

Dad winds down the window to speak to Amanda. 'Thanks for having our Em. One day we'll return the favour. We'll have a big party, when the house is done.'

Rachel bounds down the steps and gives me a hug. She looks at her mum, leaning over talking to Dad, and rolls her eyes. 'Come on.'

We leave them to it.

'So?' Rachel lolls back on the purple-and-silver sequinned bed quilt. 'How are you?'

'OK. Glad to be here.' I sit with my back against the radiator. It's the warmest I've been for about three weeks. 'The caravan is freezing. It's totally mad, us living there in the winter.'

'You could always live here for a bit,' Rachel says. 'Mum loves it when you stay over. You can share my room.'

I'm not sure how, exactly. It's a bit difficult to see how the spare mattress is going to fit, even for one night. The floor is covered in so much junk you can't see the carpet: paper, photos, files, books, shoes and bits of clothing. The desk is the same, with Rachel's computer and speakers perched on top of the piles of stuff.

Rachel sighs. 'I've got masses of coursework to finish. Have you done yours?'

"Course not,' I say. 'Anyway, it's Friday. There's loads of time.' I pick up her photography journal. There's not much in it; a few good photos of a fairground, and some we took together, at a railway station in London.

'Mr Ives said something really odd to me,' I say.

'What?' Rachel's only half listening; she's checking text messages at the same time.

'He said my photos were like Francesca's.'

Rachel looks blank.

'You know, Francesca, who is my real mother?'

'Yes, I know. But how come he does? That is weird. What else did he say?'

'Nothing else. He just moved on to the next person.'

'And you didn't ask him? Honestly, Em!'

'I was too shocked. I mean, it was so out of the blue. I only started thinking about it afterwards.'

Rachel shakes her head at me. 'You're crazy, Em. You should have just asked Ivesy what he was going on about. I've never understood it, why you aren't more curious about your real mum.'

"Cos it was all so long ago, I suppose, that she left. And she's never bothered about us. Never once. So why should we care about her?'

'Except it doesn't work like that, does it?'

I don't say anything.

'Perhaps Ivesy used to know her. Like, when they

31

were young. At art college or something. He must be at least forty. How old is Francesca?'

'Bout the same, I suppose.' My back's too hot. I wriggle forward and stuff a pink cushion between me and the radiator.

The truth is, I never think about Francesca being any age. It's hard enough to think of her being real at all. Like, a normal person, living her life somewhere.

Rachel's staring down at me from the bed, a funny expression on her face. 'Well, if she's some famous photographer we can just look her up, can't we?'

'She's not. Not famous,' I say quickly. I'm wishing I'd never mentioned it all now. Stupid.

'How do you know?' Rachel's already typing Francesca's name.

'I've already looked,' I say.

'Ah. So you are just the tiniest bit curious about her, after all.'

'There's no point, though,' I say. 'She doesn't want anything to do with me and Kat. She never has. It was fourteen years ago, Rach. She's never once contacted us. What does that tell you?'

'Well . . . there might be millions of reasons why she's not been in touch. For a start, you're always moving house. It's not that easy to keep track of you. Have you ever thought about that? You don't even have a proper address, now. *The caravan, a field.* How's she supposed to find you there?'

I don't answer. *There is a box for mail, at the caravan site. There's always ways and means of finding someone,* I could say. But I don't.

Rachel's in full flood. 'She was probably ill. That's why she left. We've done it in Psychology. Post-natal depression; that makes people do weird, awful things. My mum knew this woman with a six-week-old baby who jumped in front of a train –'

'That's too awful,' I say. 'But I wasn't a baby. I was two, when she left. And she was in love with someone else. Kat knows about it. Kat can actually remember her.'

'Supper's ready!' Amanda calls up from the kitchen.

It's a relief to go downstairs. I don't want to talk about my mother any more. I've always thought I was fine about it all, and now I find I'm not. Mr Ives' stupid remark is playing tricks with my head, stirring up stuff I hardly knew was there.

We eat the most delicious vegetarian lasagne in the whole world, and home-made chocolate mousse for pudding: Amanda is the best cook ever. She's about as different from Cassy as you could imagine. She loves cooking, and clothes, and she works in a video and DVD shop. She split up with Rachel's dad about three years ago. He's the only thing we are not allowed to talk about.

'I've got out *Two Days in Paris*,' Amanda says when we've washed up. 'Want to watch it with me? It'll be more fun for me with you two there.'

The dialogue is really funny. There's loads of sex in the film too. It's not embarrassing, watching it with Amanda the way it would be with Cassy and Dad. She's pretty relaxed about stuff.

'Perhaps we should all go to Paris for a weekend,'

Amanda says. 'The three of us, in the spring. Start saving up!'

'I need a job,' I say. 'I want to get driving lessons too.'

'I'll ask in the shop for you, if you like,' Amanda says.

Rachel looks indignant. 'What about me? I need a job more than Em. Em never spends money on anything.'

'That's why I need a job, silly. I don't have any money, that's why I don't spend any.'

'It's never stopped me!' Amanda laughs. 'Still, I'll ask around for both of you. Polly sometimes needs someone in the run-up to Christmas, in her shop. And there's the market stall too. If you two can earn enough for spending money, I'll pay for travel and a hotel in Paris.'

Just as we're dropping off to sleep (Rachel under her muslin drapes, between lilac sheets, me snuggled in a pink duvet on a pink futon mattress next to her), Rachel says, 'We should ask Mr Ives straight out, what he meant about Francesca. Find out how he knows her. What she does. Where she is. We could find her, Em. Imagine that! After all this time.'

'I don't think so,' I say. 'Just leave it, now, Rach. Please?' I turn over, pretend to be asleep. It's not long before I can tell Rachel really is asleep, and I lie there in the dark, listening to all the familiar sounds of a normal house, in a normal busy street in a town at night: radiator pipes clanking, bath water running;

sirens and traffic and voices as people go along the street; a dog barking. The street light glows orange through the bedroom curtains.

Amanda comes out of the bathroom and crosses the landing into her room; finally she switches off the radio, and the house is quiet. The street noises settle down too. But I'm still awake, thinking about Francesca, and Paris, and Rachel's take on the world. How everything to her is straightforward and simple and has an explanation.

I haven't mentioned Seb once.

By the time Rachel and I get downstairs in the morning, Amanda's already gone to work. She has left us a note, and ten pounds:

Help yourselves to breakfast: croissants in the oven, fresh grapefruit in the fridge. Buy yourselves something nice for supper: I'm going out tonight.

'Your mum's really kind,' I say.

Rachel gives me her A-level Psychology look: sort of knowing and analytical. 'She's trying to buy our love, you realise. Lots of single parents do it, to make up for not being there. Because they feel guilty.'

'You talk such rubbish,' I say.

'Shall I dry your hair?' She looks at me still wrapped up in my white towel turban, smelling of Amanda's expensive geranium and orange bath oil (*for relaxation and a sense of balance*).

'Go on, then.'

'I'm going to straighten it,' Rachel says. 'Smarten you up. I'll do your make-up too.'

By the time she's finished, I don't look like me. I purse my lips in the mirror: they're sticky with dark red lipgloss and lipliner. My eyes are ringed with black, like a cat's. I mess my hair up a bit with my hands.

Rachel watches over my shoulder. 'Leave it,' she says. 'You're spoiling it!'

We go down to the bottom of town first, to look at a jacket Rachel's seen.

We look at the stuff in the posh shops, but we only ever just look, because it's all too expensive and in any case, the clothes are probably made by child labour and Third World exploitation and all that. It's hard being ethical and fashionable. Next we go to the charity shops, because sometimes you get bargains in there.

'This looks like your sort of thing!' Rachel holds up a black vest, with a velvet edge.

I find a skirt I like too. Three pounds for them both!

'Now, coffee,' Rachel says.

We go to Madisons, upstairs in the mall, which means we go past Bob and his dog on the way. Bob's this homeless bloke me and Kat have known for ages, from when he first had Mattie as a puppy. She's a lurcher cross: smaller than your average lurcher, but skinny and beautiful.

'Hello, Bob!' I say. I give him a two-pound coin. 'For your cup of tea.'

'Thanks, sweetheart.'

I pat Mattie. She stands up, as if to be polite, and then she turns round again three times and settles back on her blanket, curled round, watching me with her beady brown eyes.

Rachel doesn't approve. 'That's why you never have any money. And he'll only spend it on booze or drugs,' she says as we go up the escalator. 'You shouldn't encourage begging on the streets.'

I don't argue. Perhaps she's right. But Bob's had a sad and horrible time, and it isn't fair, whatever she says, that he's ended up homeless. He had a family once. He told me and Kat about it. He's got a little girl somewhere he never sees. His girlfriend chucked him out and he lost everything.

We call in to see Amanda, in the video shop. She's busy at the counter, slipping DVDs into their boxes.

'You can pick a couple of films for this evening, if you like,' she says, as soon as she's finished serving.

'So, where are you going?' Rachel asks.

'Out,' Amanda says.

'With whom?'

'Mind your own bees' wax!' Amanda says, but Rachel doesn't laugh.

We choose two DVDs from the New Releases shelf. Through the archway into the second room, I glimpse the back of a slim, dark figure that looks familiar. My heart does a little skip. He's looking along the Foreign Films section. He's wearing a shabby long coat, and black jeans, and he's got a rather nice leather bag over one shoulder. I'm pretty sure it is Seb, but he doesn't turn round, and I'm not ready to tell Rachel about him, not yet . . . so I don't go up to check.

'Come on, Rach,' I say. 'Let's go and choose something nice for supper.'

She's still in a mood.

I choose the pizzas (mozzarella and rocket) and chocolate ice cream.

'Mothers! Yours and mine! What are they like?' I say in a silly voice while we're queuing for the checkout, to try and make her laugh, but that doesn't work either.

Back at her place, she goes on the computer for ages. I find a novel on the shelves they have in their bathroom (so you can read on the loo), and curl up on the squashy sofa in the living room to read it. It's about a dead girl who is in heaven and can see everything happening down on earth; how sad her parents and friends are and all that. It's quite a cool idea: I've always thought that it would be a shame to miss out on hearing all the nice things people say about you when you're dead, at your funeral. At about six I go upstairs again. Rachel's back at the computer, though the bed's all ruffled up as if she's been asleep.

'Hey, Rach,' I say. 'This is silly. Why don't we talk about it?'

'What?' she says, as if she didn't know. She still won't look at me.

'Your mum. Her going out. You feeling like crap.'

'I'm fine,' she lies. She's chatting to Luke on MSN.

'Are you getting hungry yet?' I ask.

'Yes.' She looks up, finally. 'Shall we cook?'

* * *

Finally, hours later, after the films and when we're both in bed and the lights are out, Rachel starts to talk about her mum. It's easier, talking in the dark.

'It makes me sad,' she says. 'Knowing how lonely Mum is. Seeing her going out on these stupid dates. At her age.'

'She's not that old!' I say. 'And she seems fine to me.'

'She doesn't tell me where she's going or who she's seeing. I don't really want to know, I suppose, and she knows that. Deep down, I still can't help wishing she'd get back with Dad, even after all this time.' She sniffs.

Most of the time, Rachel is bright and cheerful, and you'd never guess there was this seam of sadness underneath it all. I remember her when we were about ten, blowing out her birthday candles and making a wish, when we still believed wishes would come true. She used to have the best birthday cakes ever, home-made by Amanda, in special shapes with coloured icing, different each year: a cat, a fairy castle, and one year a leaping dolphin.

I try to put myself in her shoes, now. I try to imagine what she's feeling about Amanda, so I can understand better. It's quite hard: Dad and Cassy have always been there, as far back as I can properly remember, and my relationship with Cassy isn't like mother and daughter at all. When I think about my *real* mother, there's only a dark place, a sort of space where something ought to be.

'About Francesca,' I start saying.

I sense Rachel's listening.

'I don't feel sad, exactly,' I say. 'It's not as if I'm missing her. How can I, when I don't even remember her? There's just a hollow feeling, where she ought to be but isn't. I only started thinking about her again because of what Mr Ives said, as if I was like her in some way.'

'I expect you are angry with her, deep down,' Rachel says. 'Like when someone dies, the people left behind feel abandoned and sad, but angry too. There are lots of different stages to grief. It must be the same thing for you.'

'No, it isn't,' I say. 'I don't feel anything.'

Only that isn't quite true either, any more. Because if it was, why did I find myself looking at that book of stories she left behind? Tracing my finger over her name written in the front, as if there's a clue hidden there, if only I could look long and hard enough?

'When I was little,' I tell Rachel, 'and I shared a room with Kat, she used to tell me stories about Francesca.'

She'd whisper them to me at bedtime, dripping words into my open ears, filling my head with them. Her voice was soft, like leaves falling, laying down the memories in layers. '*Shh . . . Dad mustn't hear us talking.*' Even then, Francesca was a secret.

Rachel's quiet for a bit, then she says something I'll remember for ever. 'I think I would want to know everything about my mother. I would think it was a way of finding out something about myself. I'd want to know the ways I was like her, and the ways I was different.'

I don't say anything.

'So what things did Kat tell you, exactly?' Rachel asks.

'She said Francesca was an artist, before she met Dad. She told me that Francesca called me Emily, because she liked all the famous artist and writer Emilys. She told me that Francesca fell in love with someone, another artist, and she gave up everything for love, to follow her heart.'

I can *hear* Kat saying those words. Drip drip, in my ear.

The words are so final: like a door shutting. *Click!*

A rush of cold air. Then nothing.

Rachel sighs. 'It sounds so romantic: *everything for love. Following your heart.*'

'Not when you think what she left behind, it doesn't,' I say. 'Dad. Kat. Me. How could she do that? And if your own mother hasn't a place in her heart for you, what does that mean? What kind of mother is she? Why on earth would you ever want to find her?'

'Oh, Em!' Rachel whimpers.

Neither of us says anything else for ages. Rachel stretches out in the bed. I turn over. It's impossibly hot.

'Can I open the window?'

'I'll do it.' Rachel leans over and pushes the window wide.

A while later we hear footsteps along the path, and then the squeak of the metal gate. Keys rattling, the front door swinging open. I know Rachel's straining to listen, to find out if her mother is by herself or if she's brought someone back with her, for the night. But we don't hear voices, just the usual, ordinary sounds of Amanda hanging up her coat, kicking off her shoes, traipsing upstairs. She runs a bath. At some point she stops outside our door.

We both lie very still.

Amanda pads along the carpeted landing again to the bathroom.

Rachel lets out a long breath, as if she's been holding it for ages, waiting, and listening.

The radiators come on automatically at some early hour. The house seems stifling to me, too soft and carpeted and fussy. I just want to get back to the caravan now, even if it is so cold there. I need some fresh air. Breathing space.

'I ought to get back, soon,' I tell Rachel when she finally wakes up. 'I've got loads of work to finish today.'

'Me too.'

Perhaps she's glad to get rid of me. The weekend has been unusually intense. Too many feelings swilling around. She's seeing Luke later, in any case.

I try phoning Dad, for a lift, but he doesn't answer.

Amanda gets the bus timetable out for me. 'I wish I still had a car sometimes,' she says. 'Like now. I'd be able to take you back. Sorry, Em.'

'Still, you're helping save the planet!' I say. 'So it's good, really.'

She laughs. 'Come again soon. And I meant it about Paris. Ask your dad if it's OK by him.'

They wave me off from the front-door step. Rachel's still in her pink pyjamas. Amanda stands behind Rachel and puts her arms round her, and they rock slightly together. Mother and daughter. For the first time, looking at them so close together I notice a sort of twinge in me, a pang of something like regret.

It's spitting with rain by the time I get to the bus stop. I watch the way the wind whips the leaves off the silver-birch tree on the other side of the road: they whirl and dance, gold specks caught in spirals. It would make a good photograph. A car whizzes by too close to the kerb and splashes a puddle right up over my jeans. Finally, the bus turns up.

The heater under the seat pumps out stale warm air over my sodden jeans. I smell like an old wet dog drying out. Luckily the bus is practically empty. I start wondering where Dad and Cassy are. Perhaps they were still in bed when I phoned. Or they've gone out somewhere for the day. I hope not. For some reason, I really want to see them. Want everything to be normal, and OK.

Just before the bus gets to my stop, I'm looking out of the window when I glimpse Seb again. At least, I think it's Seb. A boy in a black T-shirt, and shorts and trainers, long dark hair soaked to his head, running in the rain along the edge of the road. I clear a bigger space in the misted-up window, crane backwards to see: he veers off the road down a track by the bridge, down towards the river, and disappears.

6

It's Friday before I can go to the house again. The place is heaving: workmen in yellow hats everywhere; a digger carving out a trench for pipes; and the whole building covered inside and out with scaffolding, so it looks like it's in a horrible cage. Nick, Seb's dad, is working on the roof.

I lock my bike against the beech tree and walk across the field to the river, away from all the noise and mess. The water is pelting along. A duck trying to swim upriver keeps getting swept back down by the current. It gives up, eventually. I take a series of photographs of the water: I'm trying to do lots of different natural forms before I choose the theme for my project. We've got to tell Mr Ives next week what we're doing. I take different angles: I want to get the texture of the moving water, and the metallic sheen where a thin shaft of sunlight hits it. I walk further along the bank away from the house and all the noise, and find a row of old willow trees twisted into interesting shapes, so I take photos of them, too and a bit of rusty old fence railing.

The other side of the river, a dark figure is running

in this direction. Black T-shirt, dark shorts. As he gets closer I can see his long hair, and this time I know for sure it's Seb.

He hasn't seen me yet. His eyes are fixed on the path, dodging the mud and the puddles. I move out from the trees, and he looks up. For a second he breaks his rhythm, and then he gets back into it. I think he's seen me, but he runs on, directly opposite me now across the river, and keeps on running. Once he's passed, further away, I focus the camera lens on him, the blurred image of a figure in movement. *Click.* And again. *Click.* I check back at the sequence of photos I've just taken. Black and white, they'd look better. I take some more of the ducks, and then some other bird, that flaps noisily up from one of the trees. Moving images. Flight. They're good, those last few pictures.

I'm just about to go back to my bike when I hear footsteps thudding along and realise Seb's coming along this side of the river. He must have gone all the way up to the bridge and then back.

He slows down, checks his watch, stops. His forehead is beaded with sweat. Mud is splattered all over his legs and shoes. He grins. 'Hello, you!'

I take a step back. 'You're all wet!'

He shakes his head, and his hair sends tiny droplets of water over me in a fine spray, like when a wet dog shakes.

'Yuck! You did that on purpose!'

'No!'

'Disgusting!'

He pulls his hair back; his face looks much thinner like that. High cheekbones, deep brown eyes. Stubble along his chin.

'So, you're not working on the house today?' I say.

'Very observant. Not today, not any day.'

'Why? What's happened?'

He looks down for just a second, as if he's ever so slightly embarrassed to tell me. 'He was getting on my nerves. Dad. Criticising all the time. He's never satisfied. We had an argument. So I packed it in. He went ballistic. Usual stuff.'

'I'm sorry.'

'Why should you be sorry?'

It's my turn to look embarrassed. 'Never mind.'

I can't tell him I'm sorry because it means I won't see him when I visit the house, can I?

I watch that stupid duck trying to swim up the river. I look at Seb again. 'So, what are you doing now?'

'Running. Obviously.'

'For work, I meant.'

He shrugs. 'Nothing. Something will turn up. Or not.'

He looks at the camera. 'More photos? School work?'

'Yes. So?' I know I sound defensive, but I hate that tone in his voice. At least I'm doing something constructive with my life.

We stand awkwardly side by side. In the distance, the digger roars and revs.

'They're getting on with it fast now all right,' Seb says.

'I liked it better, before. Now it's all noise and mess.'

Seb starts hopping from foot to foot. 'Got to keep moving.'

'Sorry. Go on, then.'

'It's OK. I mean, I chose to stop. When I saw you. I've done an hour, already. I'm going back home now, anyway.'

My face goes hot. 'So, what else are you doing, apart from running? Now you're not working?'

'Nothing much. Driving lessons. Films. Reading.'

I don't mean to look surprised, but he obviously notices something.

'You don't have to be at school to read, you know.'

'I know that.' Most people I know at school hardly read anything at all. Even people doing English with me, which is weird. But Seb? Running. Reading. I clearly don't know the first thing about him.

'Why aren't you at school, though?' I ask. 'How old are you?'

'Seventeen. No point. Hated exams, useless at them. It's all exams. There isn't anything else.'

'That's so not true! There's friends, and fun and stuff –'

'Fine. You don't need school for that, though. And it ought to be about learning, but it isn't really. People are just going through the motions. Just the little bit they need to pass exams. Then they can go to university. Pass some more exams. Get a job with a salary. Get some ridiculous mortgage. Work till they die.'

'You make it all sound horrible. But I like what I'm

47

doing. My subjects, and seeing my friends. What's wrong with that?'

'Nothing. It just doesn't suit me. Hate sitting down. Hate being inside all day. Being told when I've got to do things. Someone else bossing me about.'

'What do you like, then? If you hate all that so much? What's the alternative?'

'Playing music. Running. Sleeping. Thinking. Making stuff.'

'What sort of stuff?'

'This and that. With wood. Carpentry. Stone carving. I like that.'

'Except not with your dad.'

'Not every day. Not nine till five. Not with him giving me the most boring, easy job and then telling me I'm doing it wrong all the time. Or too slowly. Calling me a loser, just because I don't want to do some stupid job for less than the minimum wage.'

It starts to rain again. I watch the raindrops hit the river water, making silver thimbles on the surface.

'I'm going to get running again,' Seb says, 'before I freeze up. See you again.' He touches my arm, ever so lightly.

It takes me completely by surprise.

'I didn't mean to sound so harsh,' he says. 'It's just, like with my dad and that.'

'It's fine,' I say. 'I know. I understand.'

I watch him as he runs back the way he's just come, towards the bridge again. I'm already wet through; staying a bit longer isn't going to make any difference.

48

My arm seems to burn where his hand was, fizzing with energy. I put my other hand against it, to keep the feel of it there as long as possible. I wait till he's run past on the other riverbank, and then I walk back over the wet grass to my bike, and cycle home.

Cassy slams the door and collapses in an exhausted heap on the sofa, still wearing her coat.

'What's the matter, Cass?'

'I'm wiped out, that's what. Having to walk down the lane in the rain is the final straw.'

'I thought Dad was giving you a lift?'

'He had site visits. Said he'd be late again, and I couldn't bear waiting any longer in the library.'

'I'll make supper, shall I?'

'You're such a love!' Cassy flicks on the telly. She watches a bit of the news, then flips channels again. She looks too pale, as if she's going down with flu or something.

'Take your wet things off, Cass!' I put on a pan for pasta. Find a jar of sauce in the cupboard. I throw together a salad from bits and pieces in the fridge. By the time it's all ready, Cassy's asleep. I turn everything off; it will wait. The caravan is steamy from the damp clothes drying off, and the cooking. The windows are running with condensation.

Dad finally comes in at seven. 'Hey, kitten!' He kisses the top of Cassy's head. 'All right, Em?'

'You're late,' I say. 'Supper's cold.' I heat up the sauce again and stir it into the pasta. I ladle it out into bowls and carry them over to the table.

'How was your day?' Dad asks me. 'Do anything interesting?'

'No.'

'How's it all coming along? Keeping on top of your school work?'

'It's all fine, Dad.'

'You know how important it is. I was chatting to one of the stonemason chaps, at the house. His son's about your age. Just drifting along, not doing anything. He's a bright enough lad. But no sticking power.'

Cassy stretches and yawns. She takes her bowl back to the sofa to eat. 'Expect he just hasn't found the right thing yet,' she says. 'It takes some people longer than others, to find the right path. And some of us never do!'

I zone out while she goes on about her work at the library, and her friend Anita who wants to be a writer but never actually writes anything.

'Dad?' I say. 'Rachel's mum's going to take me and Rachel to Paris. She said to ask you.'

Dad glances at Cassy. 'Well,' he says, slowly.

'She's going to pay for it all,' I say. 'Everything except for spending money. So me and Rach are going to get jobs at Christmas. Then I can afford driving lessons too.'

'It's not as simple as that,' Dad says. 'For a start, Rachel's mother hasn't got the money to pay for you. It isn't right. And we've got huge expenses with the house renovation, and there's Kat to support, remember . . . It's not a good time, Emily. Your first exams are only just round the corner, in January. I

50

don't want you taking on a job.'

'Just typical!' I dump my empty bowl in the
it clatters loudly.

What I'd really like to do is flounce off into my room
and slam the door. But it's freezing in there, and you
can't slam a flimsy MDF partition, not so it makes a
loud bang like a proper wooden door.

'We'll think about it,' Dad says.

Right.

'Got homework?' Cassy asks.

'Of course.'

'You have the table, then. I'll stay on the sofa and
read. Rob can wash up, yes? For a change!'

The room seems smaller than ever, filled up with
my bad mood. Soon as he's finished crashing pots and
pans around in the stupid kitchenette, Dad comes
back in. 'Want to go for a quick drink, Cass? At the
Crown?'

'Not tonight, babe. You go. I'm too tired.'

Once he's gone, my mood shifts a bit. I show Cassy
my photos, and she says she likes them, and how
clever I am.

'I'll get round your dad, about Paris,' she says. 'Give
us a week or two.'

'And about the job?'

'That too. It'd be good for you. Somewhere else to go
at the weekend.'

'Thanks, Cassy.'

We go to bed early. It's warmer under the duvet. I
listen to Cassy sorting out the fold-down sofa bed. She
watches telly till Dad gets back at eleven.

It's the pits, living in this tiny space. It's going to drive us all crazy.

When I close my eyes, I let myself imagine our real house, finished. Those solid stone walls and big rooms and tall, beautiful windows. Under-floor heating. Huge, proper bathrooms. My own room under the roof. Acres of space.

Another thought bubbles up.

Francesca. Another house, somewhere a long way off. A house that I haven't seen and can't possibly imagine. But it's out there somewhere, for real, and Francesca is living in it. My mother, living her parallel life.

7

'When developing negatives, the film must be kept in complete darkness until the fixer is added. It can still be affected by the red "safe light", so it is placed in a light-proof bag before being extracted from the film canister . . .'

Rachel reads my notes out loud. She hasn't written hers up yet. We've been learning how to use cameras with film, as well as digital, and how to develop our own negatives (black and white). I love the magic of watching images slowly appearing on the strips, and how everything is the opposite of what you'd expect: dark where it will eventually be light.

My trees, and the river sequence, and the birds in flight have come out well.

'What's this one?' Rachel holds up the black and white photo of a blurred figure.

'I'm experimenting with movement,' I say. 'That's someone running along the riverbank.'

She peers at it more closely. 'Who, exactly?'

'Just some random person!' Why do I lie, exactly? I'm not sure; perhaps because of the way Rachel doesn't let things go. Or because it's such an early stage of me knowing Seb, it feels special and secret. There's nothing for her to get hold of in any case. Not like her and Luke, practically an item now.

Mrs Almond is taking this lesson, not Mr Ives. She's going round the tables, checking our themes for the AS-project coursework. She flips through my notebook, and then picks up the pile of new photos I've just developed and checks through them.

'Lots of good work here, Emily.' She smiles at me. 'You've done well to keep your project log up to date too. Some people,' she looks at Rachel, 'would do well to take a leaf out of your book.'

Rachel sighs dramatically. 'What kind of a mate are you? Showing me up all the time.'

'The trees are particularly interesting, technically speaking,' Mrs Almond says. 'They'd make a good study. Those silver-birch trunks, the willows and the back-lit beech tree. Stunning compositions. And perhaps you could contrast them with trees in more urban settings. Have a look at the work done by photographers like Graham – he's Canadian. And Adams, of course. You need to show the examiners you've researched the field. And find your own emotional connection to the material. Your original "take" on it.'

'How can they expect us to be original?' Rachel grumbles. 'We've only been doing Photography for about ten weeks!'

I spread out my new pictures over the table. I rearrange them, in date order of taking them. I think about doing a series of time-lapse studies: one tree, over a whole day. Or I might go back at the same time each week, from now till Christmas, and see how the light changes, and the tree too: the leaves will all have fallen by then. But what's my own connection to the material, like Mrs Almond said? The emotional link?

I work at it.

I suppose the beech tree is special because it's right next to our new house, and because it is so huge and beautiful. The birches, I just liked the look of, the way the slender trunks made silver lines, almost an abstract pattern. But there's a poem too, about birches, we read in English last summer, which I love. And Dad used to read me a poem about stopping in woods, in the snow . . . Perhaps I could cut out bits of poems about trees, and use words in some way, with the photos?

Later, waiting at the bus stop at the end of the school day, I'm still getting ideas. I'm looking at the line of sycamore trees up the school drive and that makes me think about their seeds: sycamore keys, that hang in bunches in the summer. There were sycamore trees next to the primary school and when we were in Year Three or Four we used to take the seeds and stick them on our noses and pretend to be dinosaurs.

I start remembering other things: Kat and me, making a den under an oak tree in some woods near the house we lived in when I was about nine. We piled logs up against the trunk, and wove bracken in and out like a lattice, and sat inside in the dry, listening to

55

the patter of rain on leaves and felt happy and safe . . . Now I start thinking about it, trees have always been special to me.

I'm so busy daydreaming I don't see him till I'm actually stepping on to the bus: Seb, waving at me to join him on the seat at the back. I'm so taken by surprise I go and sit down right next to him, and before I can stop myself I've blurted out: 'What are you doing here? Can't keep bumping into you like this!'

As soon as the words are out of my mouth I'm thinking how stupid and clichéd I sound. But he doesn't make a sarky comment or even give me his usual ironic look.

'I'm stalking you!' He laughs. 'Not really!'

'Oh, well, good, I suppose. That you're not a stalker, I mean!'

'I guessed you'd get this bus,' Seb says. 'I was about to catch a bus back from town, but I worked out you'd be on this one after you finished school. So I waited. I want to ask you something.'

'What?'

'I'm taking my driving test, Friday. If I pass, do you want to go somewhere with me? In the car?'

'You've got a car?'

'My mum's car. So, do you?'

'OK. Yes. Where, exactly?'

'A film or something?'

'OK.'

'So what's your mobile number?'

I tell him. He gives me his. I can hardly believe it. Seb is exchanging phone numbers with me! I don't even mind the two Year Eight girls in the seat in front of us giggling and turning round to earwig and blow bubbles with gum, making disgusting noises. By the time they get off at their stop they are practically wetting themselves.

'What's their problem?' Seb says, once they've got off.

'Being thirteen?' I say. 'Being ignorant?'

'School's full of people like that,' Seb says.

'Not in the sixth form,' I say. 'It's much better now. All those sort of people have left.'

'If you say so.'

'So, what were you doing in town?' I ask him.

'This and that.'

'You don't give much away.'

'No.'

'Got a new job yet?'

'You sound just like my dad.'

'Sorry.'

'You say sorry a lot, don't you?'

'Sorry!'

We both laugh.

The bus slows down to go over the bridge. I reach forward to ring the bell. 'Mine's the next stop.'

'The middle of nowhere.'

'Exactly.'

'What time do you have to leave in the mornings?'

'Too early. The bus goes at five to eight.'

The bus stops abruptly and jerks me forward down the aisle. 'See you! Good luck for Friday!'

I stand at the kerb as the bus draws off. Seb

waves at me from the back seat. The bus grinds up the hill: Seb's silhouetted against the lit window, still waving. My heart's all fluttery and I can't stop smiling.

Seb asked me out.

Friday we are going out together.

Seb and Em. Sounds funny.

Seb and Emily. Better.

I practise, all the way down the lane to the caravan field, under the trees.

Dad's home early. He puts his finger to his lips as I come in the door: Cassy is stretched out on the sofa, dozing.

I make tea. I take it into my tiny bedroom and lie on the bottom bunk.

'This came for you.' Dad hands me a white envelope with Kat's writing on the front. 'You're the lucky one!'

'What's wrong with Cass?' I ask him. 'She's always tired. She looks terrible.'

Dad looks surprised, as if he hasn't even noticed. 'Well,' he starts. 'She's working hard.'

'I think you should talk to her,' I say. 'Make her see a doctor.'

Dad doesn't respond to that. 'Open your letter, then,' he says. 'Tell us what Kat says.'

'Dad! No way! It's a private letter. To me.'

He smiles.

'Go away, Dad!'

I take a big slurp of tea and tear open the envelope.

* * *

Dear Em

How are you????? Bet it's even more freezing now in the caravan! Actually, York is much colder than Somerset! However, you will be dead jealous to know that not only do I have my own room with bed/desk/chair/wardrobe/en-suite shower and loo but also CENTRAL HEATING!

I am sooooo happy! I am now going out with Dan, who is this most gorgeous, über-clever guy studying Marine Biology. You would absolutely love him. He has dark hair and brown eyes and is super fit. You can look at him on my Facebook.

Plus: I got 68 for my first essay which is quite good, and 72 for the practical, which is a distinction. You can tell Dad that bit. Nothing else.

Give Cassy a big hug from me. I liked the photos you sent. You have got much better in a very short time. I showed some people here who know about art and things and they say they are really good too. You should do Photography at uni if you want to. Dad might throw a fit about it not being academic enough but it is YOUR LIFE and I think you should do a subject you really love. You can think about jobs and stuff later on. Anyway, some people get jobs taking photographs, don't they? I suppose you'd have to be, like, exceptional. But if you did it with English you could do journalism or something like that. You've always been good at writing.

A job in Polly's shop sounds cool. I have been doing part-time bar work at the students' union which is OK-ish and I need the money. Science textbooks cost silly amounts, like fifty quid EACH!!! (Don't tell Dad about the job though.)

What else is happening? Are you missing me? How is the house coming along? When will it be ready????

Have you seen that boy again at the house???? Is it nice getting a real proper−letter−on−paper from your loving big sister? Send me one sometime, or better still, a parcel with stuff in it. Dan's mum sent him one, tied up in old−fashioned brown paper and string and everyone thought it was really cool!

I might go to Dan's at Christmas/New Year. He lives in London. (But I will come back and see you too, I promise.)

Loads of love

xxxxxxxxxxx Kat

I read it twice. Just for a moment I miss Kat so much my whole body aches. I know we argue and fight sometimes but she's always been there, my whole life. I can't bear it if she doesn't come back for Christmas.

I reread that paragraph.

Dan. Last time she mentioned someone, it was Simon.

It's supper time. Dad has cooked, for once. He brings the oven tray to the table: fishcakes and chips.

Cassy sits up, bleary-eyed. 'I don't think I want anything,' she says. 'I'll just have some toast later. Sorry, Rob.'

'So how's our girl?' Dad asks me while we eat.

'She's just fine,' I say. 'Happy, working hard, she got

a distinction for some essay or something.'

Dad beams. 'That's our clever Kat!'

Later, in bed, I pull back the curtain and stare out. The darkness looks different. I wipe the steamed-up glass with a corner of the duvet cover. Thick fog has closed in round the caravan, cutting us off from the world even more completely. It swirls like smoke. Not far off, a fox barks. The sound is muffled but still distinctive: a vixen, calling. It's an eerie, strange cry. The first time I ever heard it, when I was about six, I thought it was a person in pain, screaming. We were on holiday somewhere; a cottage in the countryside, Kat and me sharing a tiny attic bedroom with faded rose wallpaper and old-fashioned pink eiderdowns.

Kat and I sat bolt upright in bed, calling Dad. 'What's that noise?'

'Sounds like someone's being murdered!' Cassy said, following Dad into the bedroom.

'Thanks for that, Cassy! It's just a fox,' Dad said. 'A silly lady fox calling for a mate.'

'Why's it silly?'

'Because she's made such a noise she's woken you both up!'

'We weren't asleep,' Kat said.

'Well, you should have been. It's very late. It's nearly ten o'clock.'

Dad tucked us back in. He left the door open when he went back out, so the light from the hall would shine in just enough to stop me being scared.

Now, lying in bed, the mist swirling outside,

listening to that strange sound of the fox calling into the night, I feel weird too. It's as if everything I know and that's secure in my life is somehow coming loose. Like a boat that's been untied from its mooring, drifting . . .

Kat's so very far away, her life taking its new shape without me. And now there's Seb. And Francesca: her shadowy presence coming closer . . .

As I slide into sleep, the cry of the fox outside in the darkness seems to move right into my head.

8

Friday, Rachel and I are having lunch in the sixth-form common room.

'You keep checking your phone,' Rachel says. 'Who is it? The new mystery man in your life?'

I snap the phone shut. 'No one,' I lie. Seb still hasn't texted. Does that mean he didn't pass his test, or that he's forgotten to tell me? Or he's changed his mind about going out?

Rachel tips coffee from the jar into two mugs. 'What did your dad say about Paris?'

'He's going to think about it. He wasn't exactly enthusiastic. He's so mean.'

'It's not as if it'll cost him anything.'

'Dad won't let your mum pay for me.'

'Why not? She wants to! She offered, didn't she? It'll be much more fun if you come with us.' Rachel picks up a disgusting old bag of sugar. The spoon hasn't been washed all term and is all crusted up.

'You'll get food poisoning,' I say, 'if you use that!'

'Nah. Sugar's a preservative. No bacteria can grow in it. Scientific fact.'

'I'll have another go at Dad. And we should get jobs

anyway. I won't tell him, then he can't say no.'

'What's up? You're not usually like this with your dad.'

'He's an idiot. Making us live in a caravan in the winter. It's insane. It's making Cassy sick already and it's not even proper winter yet.'

'Hey, Luke!'

And Rachel's gone, just like that! All her attention's focused on Luke, now. I don't mind, not really. I know that's how it is with Rach. I look at them, arms round each other. It's sweet, really. They've been going out together since the beginning of term, on and off. It's on, at the moment.

Still no message from Seb.

I could phone him?

Better to wait, though.

I'm on the way home when the text finally comes.

I passed! x

One kiss!

Well done! I text back. I think for a second. Add a kiss from me.

I've got as far as the caravan-site gate when the next text bleeps.

Pick you up at 7?

I think quickly. No way I want Dad and Cassy to know about Seb. Not yet.

Meet u top of lane near bus stop.

His reply comes straight back.

OK. xx

I save all his texts, so I can look at them again.

Three kisses in total. Three text kisses, like promises of real ones.

It takes me ages to decide what to wear. In the end, I just wear jeans, and my black top. I wash my hair, and dry it with Cassy's hairdryer. I borrow a lipgloss from Kat's old make-up bag, the stuff she left behind, even though I kind of know Seb won't notice stuff like make-up. It won't make any difference to him.

'We're going to see a film,' I say, in a generalising sort of way to Cassy. I don't specify who the *we* is, so I know she'll imagine it's Rachel and me. I don't want to actually lie to her. 'I'll get a lift home afterwards, so don't wait up.'

She's only half listening. She nods. 'Have fun.'

I'm nervous, waiting at the top of the lane. I'm too early. Every time a car comes along the main road my heart starts to skitter again, in case it's him. Then I start thinking he's not going to show up. But dead on seven, a silver Renault slows down and then brakes, and I see Seb's anxious face peering through the window. He looks so serious it makes me laugh.

He leans across the front seat to open the door for me. For a second, neither of us knows quite what to say.

'You all right?' I say. 'Why's the windscreen all misted up?'

'I can't find the demister thing,' Seb says. 'It's a bit different, driving all by myself. In the dark.'

I laugh. 'Are you sure you passed? Is it safe?'

He looks indignant. 'Yes. Of course.'

'Only joking. I'd be terrified, I think. Your mum

must trust you, though. Lending you her car and everything.'

'She's dead pleased with me. For passing something, for once. Proving my dad wrong.'

I try turning the temperature dial. Between us, we work out how to get warm air on the screen. 'That's better.'

'Mirror, signal, manoeuvre,' Seb says out loud. He pulls away from the kerb.

I choose us some music from the stack of CDs in the glove compartment. Not bad, seeing as they're his mum's choice! It starts to feel fun, us driving along together towards town. It begins to rain: soft, light drizzle. Seb has a momentary panic over getting the windscreen wipers going and they suddenly flip into extra-fast mode, beating like crazy, and it makes me laugh and laugh.

'Stop it!' Seb says, when we get to the edge of the town. 'I've got to concentrate. And you've got to help me find a place to park. I'm not very good at that, yet. It'll have to be a really big space.'

It takes about ten goes to get the car in the space and close enough to the kerb. I haven't laughed so much in ages.

At the cinema, Seb pays for both tickets. Rachel would say that definitely makes this a proper date. I offer him the money for mine anyway. It's not fair, expecting him to pay when he doesn't have a job or anything.

'It's OK,' Seb says. 'My mum's paying for us both.'

'Did you tell her about me, then?'

66

'Of course! Why wouldn't I? And anyway, we're celebrating my test, remember?'

Seb chooses the film. Spanish, with subtitles, an art-house film set in the Spanish Civil War that he seems to know all about. I don't really mind what we see, as long as it isn't horror.

'What've you got against horror?' Seb asks.

'I think about it too much afterwards. Can't get it out of my head. My imagination goes into overdrive. That's if it's good horror. If it's bad, it's just silly.'

'One of the best films I've ever seen is this really old one, *Don't Look Now*.'

'I've seen it too. That last scene, in Venice, with the red mac . . . and that creepy blind woman.'

And that amazing sex scene, I suddenly remember. Donald what's his name and Julie Christie when she was young, and the really slow, tender way they touch each other, making love, sort of soothing each other through their grief about the dead child. It was like I suddenly understood something, watching that. About making love, and how beautiful it could be, and how it could connect two people together at this really deep level. But I know all this sounds corny and there's no way I'm about to say any of it to Seb.

I can hardly focus on the film, at first, I'm so aware of sitting next to him. His shoulder's next to mine, his leg right up close to my leg, so that I can feel the warmth of it even through my jeans and his. We're at the end of a row, about halfway back. I can see his face, sideways on: his thin aquiline nose, and the dark

67

stubble round his chin. He's wearing his black wool jacket with the collar turned up. About five minutes in, he leans forward and starts struggling to take the jacket off, so I help him pull it off one shoulder, and then as he settles back, his hand sort of touches mine, and then he holds my hand properly, and all I'm thinking about for ages is whether it's all sweaty or too cold. But then I start to relax; the film really gets going and I just sink into the story.

Which is a kind of horror after all. Horrible and beautiful: one inside the other. Unbearable, because of what humans are capable of, and totally compelling, because of the way it shows a child finding her way out of the horror by creating her own imaginative world.

Seb holds on to my hand, all the way to the end.

He looks at me. 'All right?' he whispers, and I nod.

We stay in our seats until the last credits have rolled. We both want to see who wrote the music score. We're almost the last people to leave. I've got tears in my eyes, from that final scene where the girl is deep in the labyrinth, saving her baby brother. I'm too choked up to talk.

Seb doesn't speak either. I like that. I don't want to start dissecting everything straight away. I want to stay in the spell the story casts over you, when you're watching something brilliant. It's nice to think he's the same.

It's still raining when we make our way out of the cinema on to the dark street. We shelter under my umbrella, which means we have to walk close together. Everything feels amazing: the film, and Seb and me walking through the wet streets together, the street lights reflected in the puddles, the starry dazzle of car headlights.

'What shall we do now?' Seb says, when we're back in the car. 'Do you need to get straight home?'

'Can we go to Moat House?' I say. 'I want to see it in the dark, when there's no one there.'

Seb laughs. 'OK, if you really want to. Why not?'

By the time we get to the field gate and park the car the rain has stopped. The clouds are starting to clear; every so often an edge of silver moon appears. We pick our way across the sopping-wet grass.

'Have you got a key?' Seb whispers.

'It's under the stone near the door,' I whisper back.

'Why are we whispering?'

'I don't know! Because it's so quiet?'

'Or we'll wake the house ghost.'

'Don't talk about ghosts!'

We push the heavy door open. It creaks, like a stage sound effect. Seb makes a silly ghost *whoooo* noise, and I giggle.

'It's your house,' Seb says. 'You'd better show me round.'

'You've already had the grand tour, from Kat,' I say.

'That was ages ago,' Seb says. 'Everything's different now.'

There's still no electricity. With the roof on, it's darker than ever. We have to prop the front door open to let in the scraps of moonlight.

I take Seb's hand and pull him after me, describing each room as if it's finished. 'This magnificent fireplace is one of the original features of the house, dating from the fifteenth century. It has been restored by master craftsmen. And this kitchen is state-of-the-art twenty-first-century design, with huge French windows opening out on to the gardens and the river.'

I lead him to the bottom of the scaffolding, where the staircase will be.

'This takes us to the bedrooms,' I say. I stop. Seb's standing right behind me, so close I can feel his breath on my neck. Even in the dark, I know he is smiling. For a second, I think he's going to kiss me.

Want him to kiss me.

Everything seems to shift.

My world tilts.

'Well?' Seb says. 'Aren't we going up to see? The view must be amazing from up there.'

'We would,' I say. 'But there's no stairs!'

'No problem!' Seb has already started to climb. His voice comes from above me. 'There are ladders all the way up the scaffolding. It's perfectly easy.'

I think: *Dad. Hard hats. Safety rules.*

But I'm already following him up, climbing the ladders, hands holding tight either side, feeling with my feet for each rung, up to the first platform, and the next, and then finally out on to the wooden boards under the newly mended roof with its big skylight windows. In the dark, it's easier, somehow, to forget how high up we are.

We push open the nearest skylight and stick our

heads out. Above us, the dome of sky is a paler kind of dark. Big raggedy clouds race across the moon. In one clear diamond of sky there are stars.

I can see Seb's face properly now, in the moonlight. His eyes are shining. He looks different. Far beneath us the dark strip of the river winds through the silvered fields between the willow trees. I can hear the river, or is it the wind in the trees?

'Wow!' Seb says.

'This will be my room, up here.'

'Unbelievable!' Seb says. 'It's magic.'

The air's cold. We pull ourselves back in, and shut the skylight again. I shiver.

'Come here, you.' Seb pulls me towards him.

I'm shaking all over.

He puts his arms round me, and I hold on to him, and that's where we have our first kiss, up on the scaffolding under the wooden rafters of Moat House.

9

Wednesday after school, Rachel and I go to see her mum's friend Polly about jobs. Polly has this posh shop selling designer jewellery and hand-painted silk scarves, but she wants us to work on her stall at the Christmas market.

'It's loads of fun,' Polly says. 'There's a great atmosphere. If you two can do the stall every afternoon after school for the ten days of the market, that'll give me time to keep things running at the shop. Seven pounds an hour. What do you think?'

'Seven pounds each?' Rachel asks.

'Yes, darling! I know it's not much, but it's all I can afford.'

Rachel looks at me. Seven pounds is much more than we expected. 'That's OK,' Rachel says. 'We'll do it, won't we, Em?'

'Yes,' I say. 'Thanks. Great.'

'So you'll start next Thursday, soon as you can get there after school, yes? Go and have a look: they're setting the stalls up in the square near the church.'

Christmas lights criss-cross the streets, ready for the grand opening of the Christmas market when the mayor will switch them on. The square's busy with workmen putting up the wooden huts in rows, like a traditional German *Christkindlmarkt*.

Rachel's already looking at her watch. 'Sorry, Em, got to go. I told Luke I'd meet him at five.' She stops to check her reflection in the shoe-shop window on the corner.

'You look fine,' I say. 'Go on, then. Have a nice time!'

She gives me a quick hug. 'Love you!'

'Love you too!'

I watch her skip down River Street. She's the happiest she's been for ages.

Even by myself it's fun being in town, now everything's getting Christmassy. There are trees up in some of the windows already. The clothes shops all have party dresses on display. It's *soooo* much better than trudging across a muddy field to a cold caravan.

It starts to rain again. I cut back through the square and along past the covered market to the library. I might persuade Cassy to come with me for a cup of tea. I can say hello to Bob and Mattie on the way.

Only they aren't in their usual spot, in the little recess next to the big doors into the shopping precinct. Mattie's old blanket is there, folded neatly, but there's no sign of her or Bob. I go up the escalator to the library on the second floor. Cassy's not at the counter or the information point. I wander around for a while to see if she's shelving books or sorting out the computers. The library had a makeover in the summer: comfy seats, carpets, new computers and loads of CDs and DVDs you can borrow for a whole week for less than it costs for one night at the rental place where Amanda works. It's buzzing with people now you're actually allowed to talk in there.

Anita's at the computer desk. She smiles at me. 'Hello, Emily!'

'Can I go on the computers?' I ask her.

'Help yourself,' she says. 'There's one free in the corner. I'll just log you on.'

'Is Cassy around?' I ask.

'I don't think she's got back from her appointment yet. But I'll check for you.'

What appointment would that be, exactly? My mind starts racing. Doctor? Hospital? Perhaps there really is something wrong with Cassy. While I'm on the computer I type in some symptoms, just to see what comes up. *Tiredness. No energy. Lack of appetite* . . .

'Hey!' Cassy's suddenly right there, looking over my shoulder at the computer screen. 'Is something wrong?'

'Not with *me*,' I say pointedly, but Cassy doesn't take the hint. I click off the NHS site. 'I'm fine. Just killing time. Do you want a cup of tea with me? To celebrate me getting a job?'

'Yay! Well done, Em!' Cassy hugs me. 'At Polly's shop?'

'At the market stall. It's after school, and all day one Saturday and Sunday. Seven pounds an hour.'

'Fantastic!'

'So, tea?'

Cassy pulls a sad face. 'I can't, Em. Sorry. I've been out – had my break already. I've got to work another hour. Rob's picking me up at six fifteen. You can have a lift too, if you want to hang around till then.'

She's not going to tell me about the appointment, clearly. I study her face. She actually looks fine, now. Bright-eyed, happy even.

'I'll pay for your tea,' she says. 'Go and get something to eat too. You're looking much too skinny these days.' She disappears into the back room they use as an office and staffroom, and then returns with a five-pound note. 'There. Have a panini or something nutritious.'

'I'll have a big slab of chocolate cake,' I say, to wind her up.

I'm about halfway through my hot chocolate and raisin and oat cookie when the *click-clicking* sound of a dog's toes on the tiled floor makes me look up. Dogs aren't really allowed upstairs in the shopping centre. Mattie is skulking along just outside Madison's cafe, sniffing the air. She wags her tail when I call her name softly, but she keeps her tail low, as if she knows she shouldn't be here and doesn't want to draw attention to herself.

'Where's Bob?' I ask her.

She pricks up her ears and comes close to the railings which separate the cafe from the corridor. She whines at me.

There isn't any sign of him. I wrap up the rest of my cookie and finish my drink and go out of the cafe into the corridor. Mattie comes up and sits down close to my feet, sort of nestling in. Something's wrong. I've never seen her without Bob close by before.

When I try to coax her back down the escalator she won't come. She follows me to the top of the stairs next to the library but she won't go down the stairs either, even when I tempt her with raisin and oat cookie. She licks her lips and looks sorrowfully at me, but she won't budge.

The next minute, everything erupts. An ambulance siren gets louder and louder; the plate-glass window at the front of the shopping centre fills with blue flashing light.

Two ambulance men run up the stairs carrying a stretcher, push past me and Mattie, and go through the swing doors into the library. And just before the doors swing back behind them, I see this person lying on the floor on the carpet just inside the library foyer. I know those tatty brown cord trousers, the lace-up boots and second-hand postman's coat.

Oh, Mattie! I put my hand on her neck, to hold her back. She strains towards the door, as if she wants to get to him. I don't know what to do. I try to push the door open again.

'No entry to the library at the moment,' a security guard says. 'You'll have to come back later.'

'I need to see Cassy – she works in the library,' I try to say, but he's not having any of it. He won't listen.

'Get out of the way. There's been an incident.'

I get a glimpse of the ambulance men doing something to Bob – a mask on his face – before the security man's boot closes the door again.

Now what?

I still can't make Mattie budge. I try phoning Cassy, but her mobile's switched off. Next minute, the doors are flung back and the ambulance men go through with Bob strapped on to the stretcher, and a crowd of library staff following behind. Cassy's carrying Bob's scruffy old bag.

'Em! Wait there! I'll be back in a minute!' Cassy says as they rush past.

I sit on the step with my arm round Mattie, even though she is a bit smelly and flea-ridden. The ambulance siren starts up again. A crowd of people push forward to get a look through the window.

Footsteps trudge back up the stairs: Cassy plonks herself down next to me and bursts into tears.

'What's happened?'

'Oh, Em, it was horrible. Bob just keeled over. I think he must have had a heart attack or something. He looked awful. All grey and shaky.'

'What shall we do about Mattie? We can't just leave her here.'

'I don't know – we'll have to call the police, I suppose. They'll take her somewhere safe.'

'Where, though? How will Bob get her back? He'll be worried sick!'

'I don't know, Emily! There's nothing more we can do.' Cassy starts crying again: big, juddering tears like a little child.

Beside me on the top step, Mattie stretches herself

out with a big sigh and puts her nose on her paws. She's trembling.

'We can't just hand Mattie over to some police person who won't care about her,' I say. 'Anything might happen to her. We owe it to Bob. I'm going to phone Dad.'

It's pretty hard getting Mattie into the car. She digs her heels in. In the end Dad has to lift her into the boot.

I fetch her old blanket from the alcove, to make her feel at home.

Cassy screws up her nose. 'It's disgusting, it stinks and it's covered in fleas. Just like Mattie, in fact. We can't take her home with us, Emily.'

'We can drop her off at the police station,' Dad says. 'They deal with lost dogs all the time. They have a special dog warden.'

'Mattie's not lost,' I say.

'Homeless, then.'

'That's not her fault. If the dog warden gets his hands on her he might not let Bob ever have her back, when he comes out of hospital.'

'If,' Dad says, under his breath.

'They might give her away or have her put down or anything! It's not fair. Why can't we keep her, just till we know how Bob is?'

Bit by bit I wear them down.

Dad stops off at the supermarket on the way back. I put a bag of dry dog food and some tins in the trolley, and choose a collar and lead for Mattie. She's only got a bit of string round her neck at the moment.

'Just for tonight, then,' Dad says. 'And she'll have to sleep outside. She'll stink the place out. She'll be fine. She's used to being out in all weathers.'

'But she has Bob for company,' I say. 'She'll be lonely and cold all by herself. We could wash her? Then she won't smell so much.'

'No!' Cassy says. 'Absolutely no. One night only, tied up outside. While we think what to do. I'll phone the hospital in the morning and see how Bob is.'

Later, in bed, I phone Seb to tell him what has happened.

'I always wanted a dog, when I was little,' he says. 'But Dad wouldn't let us.'

'What are you doing tomorrow?' I ask.

'Nothing much.'

'You could come over,' I say. 'After school. We could take Mattie for a walk.'

'OK,' Seb says. 'I could meet you from school, if you like? Get the bus with you. Mum needs the car for work, otherwise I'd drive.'

'I've got a job now too!' I say.

Seb doesn't talk much after that. I guess he feels bad or something, about not having a job himself. But he says he'll meet me at three thirty. At the bus stop.

All night I keep waking up, imagining I can hear Mattie whining. She'll be missing Bob. Or freezing to death in the big cardboard box we gave her under the tarpaulin next to the bikes. I half expect to find in the morning that she's chewed through the lead and run off, trying to find her way back to Bob, like in *The Incredible Journey*. I don't hear the fox.

I think about Seb, wasting his time at home all day, not doing anything. It's not good for him. He should be doing A levels or training or something, not just lazing about. But I can't say that to him. He'd go mad. I sound just like his parents.

I start thinking about our first kiss. I replay the scene. That tingly, amazing feeling of his mouth soft against mine. The feel of his body, so close I can feel his heartbeat.

I'll see him tomorrow.

10

I'm waiting at the bus stop wondering what's happened to Seb and whether he got the bus back in town or something, when the silver Renault pulls up.

'Hop in quick. I'm not supposed to park at a bus stop.'

The Year Eight girls waiting in the queue collapse into their usual fit of giggles. One of the boys does a stupid wolf whistle.

'They're so dumb, aren't they?' Seb says. 'What's the matter with people that age?'

'Hello to you too,' I say.

'Sorry. Hello, Em.' He pulls away from the stop and does a three-point turn in about five goes. He grins. 'There. Not bad, eh?'

'Brilliant. Couldn't do better myself,' I say. 'I thought your mum was working?'

'She got back early. So I could borrow the car. She's nice like that.'

'What does she do? Her job, I mean.'

Seb glances at me. 'Care worker. What is it with you? You're obsessed with jobs. Work.'

I don't say anything. Are we about to have our first

row? I don't say what I'm thinking, which is that I'm *not* obsessed about work. I was just curious about his mum. And actually he's the one with the problem, if it comes to that. About not working. Hypersensitive or something.

'How was school?'

'Fine. How was your day?'

'Lovely.'

'What did you do?'

'Went for a run. Read.'

'What?'

'A book about the Spanish Civil War. And I just finished Cormac McCarthy's *The Road*.'

I'm impressed, of course. He reads much more widely than I do. I don't tell him, though.

'So,' Seb says, 'where shall we walk the dog?'

'Down by the river? Or we could walk from the caravan, across the fields? I'll have to change first. Get my wellies.'

We've got to the lane. Seb turns off down the tunnel of trees.

'Stop just before the gate,' I say. 'Park in the lay-by.'

We walk across the field together. The lights are on in the caravan, and there's no sign of Mattie or her cardboard box.

I open the door. This isn't how I planned things. Cassy's already home, or perhaps she's never been to work: she's curled up asleep on the sofa under a blanket, and Mattie is stretched out on the swirly orange carpet next to her. She wags her tail nervously, as if she might be in trouble, stretches, yawns and sits up.

Cassy opens one eye, sees Seb behind me, opens both eyes and sits up, startled. 'Oh!'

'This is Seb. We're going to take Mattie for a walk,' I gabble. 'I thought you'd still be at work.'

Cassy's flustered for a moment, then gathers herself together. 'I didn't go, in the end,' she explains. 'I felt I couldn't leave the dog alone all day. I had a bit of a headache.'

'Shall I make some tea?'

'Lovely,' Cassy says. 'Hello, Seb.'

'Seb's dad is one of the builders at the house,' I say. 'He helps there too, sometimes.'

'Ah. I thought I recognised you.'

'So, have you phoned the hospital? How's Bob?' I say.

'It took hours. Eventually I got through to the right ward. It's not good news. He's very poorly. Heart attack. What with sleeping rough, the alcohol: his immune system's not much good.'

'When will he be coming out?'

'Not for a long while. So we can't keep the dog. I've phoned the dogs' home. They'll keep Mattie for a while. We can still visit her and take her for walks now and then. It's the best I could think of.'

Mattie knows we're talking about her. She puts her head on one side, as if she's listening.

Seb strokes her head. 'She's lovely,' he says. 'Shame you can't keep her.'

'Can't we? Please?'

'There's no way,' Cassy says. 'We've no room. Look at this place! And you can't leave a dog alone all day while you're at work. It's not fair.'

'How come you let her inside?' I say.

'It was raining. She looked so sad. I felt bad. It's just till tomorrow.'

While I'm making tea in the kitchenette, Cassy asks Seb lots of questions about the house. He sounds quite knowledgeable, about getting the new limestone, and how you make a drystone wall. I look at them, sitting up at the table together. They're getting on really well.

'Should we feed Mattie?' I call.

'Good idea,' Cassy calls back. 'And do it outside, please. The smell of that dog food makes me sick.'

'Cassy's really nice!' Seb says as we walk back up the caravan field to the car. Mattie trots between us.

'You sound surprised.'

'No. Not really. She's younger than I expected.'

'She's not my real mother.'

'I know. You told me that before. How old is she?'

'Thirty-one.'

'How old's your dad, then?'

'Forty-two.'

'And your real mum?'

'I don't know – forty? We don't see her,' I say quickly, so he doesn't ask me anything else.

Mattie hops into the back of the car as if she's been doing it all her life.

'She's a fast learner,' I say. 'She wouldn't do that a day ago.'

Seb drives us to a place near the river, where we

can get on to the footpath that runs along it. It seemed pitch-dark when we were in the car, but when we're outside, walking along, our eyes adjust enough to make out the way. The path's too narrow to walk together: I go in front and Seb follows behind. Once we're far enough away from the road I bend down to unclip Mattie's lead, so she can run free.

'Is that a good idea? Are you sure she'll come back?' Seb asks.

'Yes. Well, I think so,' I say. 'She knows me.'

'What's going to happen to her, now?'

'Bob will have her back when he comes out of hospital. The dogs' home people will look after her till then. That's what Cassy says. But I'm worried they won't let him take her back, when they see what he's like. Homeless, no address.'

Seb shrugs. 'Well, it's not up to them how he lives, is it?'

'You should see how careful they are before they rehome an animal. They interview you and everything, to make sure you're suitable. We weren't allowed to rescue a kitten, way back, because no one was at home in the daytime.'

'If you could just keep her at Moat House, there wouldn't be a problem.'

'No. But we won't be living there till the summer.'

We've almost reached the house, on the other side of the bank. From here, it looks huge. The scaffolding makes it look bigger, perhaps. I still can't believe we'll ever actually be living here for real. It hits me, suddenly, how isolated the house is, miles from anywhere. I'm going to have to learn to drive.

'Why've you stopped?' Seb asks.

'Just looking.'

'You can see why it's called Moat House,' Seb says. 'From here, the river looks like a real moat round a castle.'

Seb takes my hand and pulls me back towards him. We stand very close. Ahead of us, Mattie stops too. She's watching the birds: hundreds of them, standing on the grassy islands of higher ground in the flooded field. The water shines like silver.

'Brent geese,' Seb says. 'Winter migrants. Just arrived.'

A blast of wind sends a flurry of silver-backed leaves from the willows growing along the river-bank. The leaves are like fish: shoals of minnows. I pull my camera out of my bag, but there's not enough light, even with a really long exposure, to take photographs.

'You take that camera everywhere, don't you?' Seb says.

'Of course. That's how you get the best shots.'

'You should take some of the dog. And the house too, as a work in progress.'

'That's Dad's job. His project, not mine.'

Seb turns his collar up. 'It's freezing,' he says. 'Shall we go back?'

I call Mattie. She stops, turns, trots obediently back. 'See? I was right! She did come when I called her. You needn't have worried!'

'We could go to my place,' Seb says. 'It's small, but

there's more space than your caravan. Mum won't mind the dog, and Dad won't be home yet.'

It's interesting seeing people's houses for the first time. Like you get to see a bit more of them. Seb's house is made of stone (not a surprise), semi-detached, at the edge of a rundown village I didn't even know existed.

'We lived near Weymouth before,' Seb says as he parks the car. 'But at least this house has a proper garden.'

We go through the garden at the side to the back door, which leads through a wooden porch into a big kitchen with a red-tiled floor and a wooden table and chairs.

Seb's mum's cooking at the stove. She turns round and smiles at me. 'Hello! You must be Emily? Yes? And who's this?' She bends down to pat Mattie, who cowers behind me.

'Mattie. She's a bit shy,' I say, 'and very muddy. Sorry.'

'She can dry out near the radiator,' Seb says. 'I'm going up to change.'

I unlace my muddy boots and leave them with Mattie next to the radiator.

'Seb's told me about you. And I've met your dad before, of course, in the pub with Nick, after work. I know he's very proud of his clever daughters.'

I don't show her I'm surprised. It's never occurred to me that Dad goes to the pub before he comes home, and that's why he's often late. It doesn't seem fair on

Cassy. It's his fault we're living in the stupid caravan in the first place, so he could at least be there as much as we have to.

'Cup of tea? Or something to eat?' Seb's mum's chopping vegetables now and the kitchen stinks of leeks, plus wet dog. 'I've got the kettle on.'

'Tea would be good. Thanks.'

I pull out a chair and sit down at the kitchen table while I wait for Seb. It's all cosy and warm. Mattie rests her head on my feet.

'You can call me Avril,' she says. 'Everyone does. Fetch me down three mugs from the cupboard, love.'

I choose three blue spotty china mugs and put them on the table.

'He's had a bit of a rough time, our Seb. He didn't get on with school. But he's bright as a button, any fool can see that. Always got his head in a book. He could do anything. If he'd put his mind to it.' She pours water into a big blue china teapot. 'But he can't seem to focus where work's concerned. Won't stick at a job. He doesn't take kindly to criticism and his dad can't stop himself. Perhaps being friends with you will give him a bit of an incentive. Like, a little nudge, in the right direction. Here's hoping!'

'What?' Seb's suddenly standing in the doorway. 'What are you telling Em?'

'Nothing at all. We're getting to know each other. Tea's ready.'

Avril must be nearly fifty. She isn't like the other mothers I know, friends' mothers I mean. She's more of an old-fashioned mother, who cooks and cleans and does everything round the house and garden. When I say this to Seb, upstairs in his bedroom, he defends her.

'It's because my dad does heavy manual work,' he says. 'And he works long hours. So he needs her to be like that. Don't knock it.'

'I wasn't,' I say. 'I was just noticing, that's all.'

'You should meet my Auntie Ruby. She's like Mum but a hundred times more so. She lived in the Welsh valleys, before the mining jobs ran out. Then they moved to Portland. She thinks it's a woman's work to look after the man and the house.' Seb notices my face and laughs. 'I don't think that, in case you're wondering!'

Seb's room feels very different from the rest of the house. He's painted the walls deep red, and there are stacks of books on shelves all along one wall. There's a bed, desk, computer and all the usual things: racks of CDs, DVDs, iPod speakers. He's got mostly foreign films, arty stuff. Indie bands. Lots of books, non-fiction mostly: history, archaeology, natural history. Which, I guess, explains how he always seems to know the names of things: *buzzard; brent geese; limestone.*

'I like your room,' I say. I finish my tea and lean back on the bed and Seb joins me. We lie there, close together, and he leans over and kisses me.

'What if your mum comes in?'

'She won't.'

I still can't relax.

'I ought to get back soon,' I say in the end. 'I've got homework for tomorrow.'

Seb sighs and sits up. 'School,' he says. 'It rules your life.'

'It's better than doing nothing all day,' I say.

Big mistake. I realise instantly I shouldn't have let the words out. Seb looks really fed up.

He gets off the bed. 'I'll drive you home,' he says, without looking at me. 'Get the dog, while I find the car keys.'

I so wish I hadn't said it. Seb hardly speaks all the way home. I kiss him goodbye, and he goes through the motions, but it doesn't feel like it did before. I've spoilt everything, and it's only the second time we've been out!

'I'll phone you tomorrow,' I say. 'Thanks for the walk and driving me home and everything.'

He strokes Mattie's head when he lets her out of the back seat. 'See ya, dog.'

I try to think what to say to Seb, to make him feel better. But I can't, and anyway, he's driving off before I get a chance to say sorry. I feel horrible.

And now there's Mattie to think about: tomorrow she'll be gone. It makes me sad all the rest of the evening, the idea of her locked up in some sort of cage, in the dogs' home, all alone and afraid.

I try one more time. 'Please, Cass. I'll feed her and take her for walks and everything. I promise. She's so good. She won't be any trouble. At least till the weekend. Bob might be out by then.'

I can see Cassy is wavering. She lets Mattie rest her head in her lap. She smoothes her soft head and pulls her ears absent-mindedly while she watches the telly.

90

I start my photography homework.

Dad gets in soon after. He comes to look over my shoulder at the computer screen. 'They're pretty good,' he says. 'Interesting topic.'

I tell him about my project. I think about what Mr Ives said, about Francesca. I watch Dad's face, waiting for a flicker of something that might show me he's thinking of her too.

And he does look wistful, for a second. But what he says is on a totally different tack.

'You're so grown-up, suddenly,' he says. 'You and Kat, both. Still, I always knew you were only on temporary loan.'

'What do you mean?' I say. 'You make me sound like a library book!'

'I mean being children – young people – you don't *belong* to your parents. You're just with us for a while. Passing through, on the way to growing up.'

'That's a bit deep, Dad!'

I'm not sure I like him thinking about me like that. As a temporary thing. I know what he means, sort of. But I also want to think I *do* belong to him. Isn't that what a family is? People belonging to each other?

'I hear you've made friends with Nick's son. Seb.'

Cassy looks up.

'And?' I say to Dad. 'What of it?'

'Nothing.' Dad hastily backtracks, as if he's embarrassed. 'He seems a nice enough lad. I thought I could invite him to the office sometime. You know, show him around. Talk to him about architecture. Might spark something.'

'Dad,' I say. 'No. Please. Just leave him alone, OK?'

Cassy's gathering her towel and stuff ready for the trek over to the shower block. Mattie gets up to follow her. I wait till the door shuts behind them.

'Did Cassy tell you about my job too?'

'Yes. She thinks it's a good idea. I'm not sure –'

'It'll be fine, Dad. It's only for ten days. It'll be good for me.'

'That's what Cassy says.' He opens the fridge and gets a beer out. 'We haven't talked much for a while, have we? Just you and me.'

'No.'

'I'm sorry about the caravan.' Dad looks ridiculous, with a pale moustache of froth from the beer. 'I know it's tough, living here.'

'It's Cassy you should be thinking about,' I say. 'It's making her ill.'

Dad looks shocked, as if it's never occurred to him before.

'She's white and sick and always tired,' I say. 'Haven't you noticed?'

Dad puts the beer down on the table. He stares at the can. He doesn't say anything for ages.

I carry on sorting my photos, and before long Cassy's back, all damp and shiny-looking from her shower, Mattie padding softly behind her, and it's time for everyone to get ready for bed.

Mattie sleeps inside the caravan, this time.

11

To: katkin
From: emilywoodman2

So much to tell you!

Can't wait for you to get home! (When???? Give me a date.)

News. We have a dog (only on temporary loan) – Mattie, remember? Bob collapsed in the library and is in hospital, so we are looking after her, but only till the weekend 'cos Cassy says there's not enough room. True, but I LOVE Mattie, she's sweet and sad and so good and obedient. I think Cassy likes her too really but Cassy is being a bit odd.

Other (main) new thing to tell you: I am going out with Seb! (hopefully NOT temporary!!!) It has been one week and two days now. We went to see a film at the weekend. Yesterday we went for a walk together, and I met his mum. I really, really like him. A lot. I can't quite believe this is happening to me. It feels weird and also wonderful at the same time. But I think I'm not very good at it, going out with someone I mean: I say things too quickly and Seb's a bit moody. I know, I know. I'm usually the moody one.

Oh, and I've actually got myself a job! Dad doesn't seem to mind too much. He is a bit preoccupied. I start work tomorrow.

It has rained here SO much. The fields are flooded.

How r u? Please send me a message. You haven't texted or emailed for ages.

xxxxxxxxxxxxxxxxxxxxxxxxxxxxxxxxxxx

From: katkin
To: emilywoodman2

Hi Em. Oh my God!!!!!! You and the beautiful boy!!! That is so amazingly cool and I'm even a tiny bit jealous (well, not really. I do have the gorgeous Dan after all). And I am a bit surprised too. Not in a horrible way because I know how lovely you are and everything, but just because I never thought you were that interested. Does that sound mean? It's not meant to.

Guess what? It's actually snowed here! We went Christmas shopping in the snow!! How cool is that?

It didn't settle or anything, though, and now it's raining. We are doing a Secret Santa thing for everyone in the flat before we all go home for the holidays.

What is going on with Cassy?

Who the hell are Mattie and Bob?

What do you want for Christmas? I don't have much money so it has to be something cheap.

Dan's old girlfriend (she's not 'old' – his ex) will be around in the holidays when he goes back to London, so I'm not sure what to think. Hmmmm. They went out together for ages, like more than a year, and split up when they went to different universities. I think it's possible she still likes him.

What's happening at the house? When will it be ready??

Just remembered about who Bob is. Honestly, Em, only you would have an old crusty dog like that.

Gtg. Making mince pies and have to write Biology essay by tomorrow.

x Kat

*How could you forget Mattie and Bob? Has your
brain erased all memory prior to uni experience???
(Rachel calls this Selective Amnesia.)*

*I am sending you a photo of Mattie (quite good but
would be better without flash).*

*Moat House now has a roof and doors and windows,
and half a staircase!*

*Why don't you bring Dan HERE for Christmas? Safe
from clutches of old girlfriend, and I get to meet him
and see if he is good enough for you.*

*(I know, million reasons why NOT: caravan too
small. Cold. No privacy. Dad being embarrassing.
Etc., etc.) BUT he could bring a tent and thermal
underwear (ha! very sexy!). What is he like? Send
photo.*

*Would you prefer 1. earrings? Or 2. silk scarf? (For
Christmas.) I can get a discount.*

xxx Em

I wait. No reply pops up. She's gone to make the
mince pies or whatever.

I have another look at the photos of Mattie. She

looks so cute with her sweet face, sad eyes, her soft ears that fold down at the top. If I print one off, Cassy can take it with her when she goes to see Bob in hospital after work tomorrow. He must be worrying about her.

Today is our first day at work at the Christmas market, after school.

'You watch the bags and scarves at the front, to make sure no one nicks anything,' Rachel says, 'and I'll keep an eye on the jewellery.'

The market's packed. We've had loads of people buying stuff already: earrings and the big bright baskets, mostly, and one guy who bought three identical pink silk scarves for *the three different ladies in my life*. Yuck. Rachel pulls a face and it's all I can do to stop myself throwing up.

'Arrogant git,' Rachel says, once she's taken the money off him. 'He's not even good-looking.'

'Perhaps he's very wealthy,' I say. 'More likely, he's got three aunties, not three girlfriends!'

It's a bit quieter while people go off to watch the lady mayor switch on the lights. The Salvation Army band starts playing Christmas carols round the huge Christmas tree in front of the church.

Rachel and I mess about, trying on the expensive hand-embroidered silk scarves. Polly said we could wear one each, to model them. It makes more people buy them, apparently. Rachel chooses a turquoise silk one. She makes me try something bright: *not your usual black*. So I end up looking like a Christmas parcel, wrapped in orange and shocking pink.

'Wow! Didn't recognise you two gorgeous girls!' Cassy suddenly appears, smiling at us. She hands us each a plastic cup of hot spiced apple juice. 'To warm you up!' she says.

'What are you doing here?' I say.

'Rob and I thought we'd come out for the evening,' she says. 'We'll be at the Jazz cafe later, if you want a lift home?'

'Aw!' Rachel says, when Cassy's disappeared through the crowds again. 'Isn't she nice to you?'

'Suppose,' I say. 'I could easily have got the bus.'

'Isn't your mystery man coming to collect you, then?'

My cheeks go hot. 'Seb? No.'

'You haven't fallen out already?'

'No.'

Have we? He was really pissed off with me, for saying that stuff. I just didn't think. But he shouldn't be so sensitive. I don't tell Rachel what happened. I'm still keeping Seb to myself. Don't want her analysing everything the way she does.

'How do these look?' Rachel preens in front of the mirror hanging at the side of the stall, checking out a necklace of chunky green beads.

'Good. Very fetching,' I say. 'Put on the matching earrings too.'

It's more like dressing up and playing, than work. We're getting paid seven pounds an hour each for having fun! And Polly's right: whatever Rachel and I are wearing, we sell more of. So we sell lots of orange scarves, and bright pink ones, and turquoise ones, and chunky necklaces. Mostly to middle-aged men. How weird is that?

At closing time, we count up the money. We've taken over two hundred and sixty pounds.

'Blimey!' Rachel says. 'Who'd have thought it!'

We have a laugh with the security men, who seem to find the idea of *roast chestnuts* very amusing.

'Don't ask,' Rachel says to me.

People begin to drift off. The street cleaners arrive to sweep up the piles of litter. We pack up all the scarves and stuff into boxes, like Polly showed us, and close the wooden doors at the front of the stall and padlock them.

Rachel's supposed to be taking the money home with her for safe-keeping, so I walk with her back to her house, in case she gets mugged or something.

'Coming in?'

'Nah. Going to meet Cassy and Dad and get my lift.'

'See you at school tomorrow, then.'

I zigzag back through the narrow streets at the bottom of town to the Jazz cafe. The streets are still buzzing with late-night shoppers. I go past the crowd of homeless people huddled on the steps waiting for the night shelter to open. Most of them have got dogs: quiet, well-behaved ones, like Mattie. I wonder about that, the way the dogs always seem contented. Perhaps they like the company. Or the freedom, being outside all day. Perhaps their owners give them lots of love and attention.

I spot Dad and Cassy through the cafe window

before they see me. It's strange just catching sight of them like that, framed in the lit window, their heads bent towards each other, engrossed in talking. It's as if I see them properly, as they are, instead of through the normal filter of my own relationship with them. He's holding both her hands across the table, and then he leans over and kisses her. They look happy.

I feel almost awkward, going in to join them. It's a strange feeling.

'Ah! There you are!' Dad looks up and grins. 'I hear you were doing a roaring trade.'

'Yes.'

'Want something to eat? Or a drink or something?' He pulls over a chair, so I can join them at the table for two.

'I'd rather get home. Unless you two want to stay longer?'

'I'll just go to the loo,' Cassy says. 'Won't be long.'

Dad shifts round to face me. 'Tired?'

I nod.

'Cassy's been a bit upset. She went up to the hospital after work. To visit the homeless bloke.'

'Bob.'

'Him. Yes. But they wouldn't let her see him. He has some infection or something. He's pretty sick. They've put him in a room by himself. So Cassy and I had a long chat about the dog, and we decided we really can't keep her, Em. I'm sorry . . .'

'And?'

'So we dropped her off at the dogs' home. On the way over here, tonight. I know you'll be disappointed.

But it's the best thing, in the circumstances.'

How dare he say that?

I hate you, I want to shout. *You tell me here, in a crowded cafe, so I can't make a fuss. Coward.*

Dad waits for me to say something. But I won't.

'I'm sorry, Em, but please don't go upsetting Cassy even more.'

It's a horrible betrayal. I'm furious with them both. And the fact that Cassy was being all nice when she came over to the stall, when in reality she'd just got rid of Mattie . . . it's unbearable.

'We can visit her,' Cassy says in the car on the way home. 'Take her for walks whenever we want. I've registered us, so we can just turn up there and take her out.'

I don't say a word all the way back. I don't speak to them at the caravan either. I go to bed without saying goodnight.

I send Seb a text.

Dad is so mean. Has put Mattie in the dogs' home. I am so sad. Didn't even say goodbye to her.

I wait, but he doesn't reply.

I cry into the pillow.

I hate everyone. Living here is shit.

12

Kat got back from university tonight.

She came via London, with Dan, and then caught another train here, and Dad picked her up from the station. We had supper together late, all together, even though I am still not talking to Cassy and Dad.

Now Kat and me are in bed. Talking in the dark, like the old days.

It's just as well we're used to sharing a room. You can hear every sniff and sigh and creak as one or other of us turns over in the bunk beds or reaches out for a drink of water.

'The thing is,' Kat says, 'Dan's bound to see her. She's back from her university, and they live, like, only minutes away from each other. They'll be getting together with old school friends. There will be parties.'

'That doesn't mean that they'll get back together again,' I say. 'They might see each other, but so what? They split up for a reason. Now he's going out with you. So I don't see why you're so worried.'

'You don't understand,' Kat says. 'He might just be tempted. You know, after a few drinks, feeling all happy and Christmassy . . . just sort of slip back into it . . . seeing as I'm not around. Out of sight, out of mind.'

'If he really likes you, he's not going to treat you like that, is he? And if he does, if he's that fickle and unfaithful, he's not worth it. You'd be better off without him.'

Kat sighs dramatically. 'It's not that simple, Em.'

'Isn't it? Why not?'

'If you don't know, how can I explain? You can't just turn feelings on and off, because of how someone else behaves! He's probably with her right this minute. It's too awful!'

'That's a rubbish way to think, Kat!'

'You don't have a clue, do you? You're too young, I guess.'

'Oh, for heaven's sake!' I turn over, in a huff.

We're both silent for ages. I kind of know she's lying on her back, staring up into the darkness, wide awake. I can feel how awake she is! And even though I'm pretending to be fed up and asleep, she knows I'm not really. That's how close we are, my sister and me.

'Do you love him?' I ask her, eventually.

'I don't know,' she says miserably. 'I don't know how to tell if it's real love, or something else. I think I do, but then why am I so scared? Why can't I trust him?'

'Is it because of how you are, or something to do with him?' I say. 'Trusting people is sometimes hard if you're not sure of yourself . . . Or perhaps because you like him so much, you're scared of losing him.' I know I sound too much like Rachel. It's not going to help Kat.

I wish I could talk to her about Seb and me, but it's not the right moment. She hasn't asked me anything about him, yet. I know she's too sad and anxious and caught up in her own stuff. The weird thing is, I feel for the first time as if I'm older than her. Wiser, even.

Kat's voice comes again out of the dark silence. 'And then there's Cassy.'

'What do you mean? What about Cassy?' My heart starts beating extra fast. What has Cassy said? I shoot straight into mad overdrive thinking about serious illnesses – *leukaemia. Multiple sclerosis. Brain tumour.*

'Don't tell me you haven't noticed? Honestly, Em!'

'What? Noticed what? What did Cassy tell you?'

'Nothing, yet. But it's obvious, stupid! She's pregnant!'

I almost fall off the top bunk.

It has really never crossed my mind. I feel totally stupid. Because it makes complete sense, now I start thinking back over things. Little bits of evidence that add up. How tired she is. Not eating breakfast. Getting upset about stuff. The appointment. Dad and her holding hands.

Instead of it being a relief, that she's not seriously ill and about to die or whatever, this huge weight comes crushing down on my chest, so I can hardly breathe.

Dad and Cassy and a new baby.

The new family, for the new house.

Kat and me: temporary loan.

Time's up.

'Well? Say *something*,' Kat says.

'Did Dad tell you?' My voice comes out small and pathetic.

'No. But tomorrow I'm going to ask them both straight out.' Kat sounds so cross and so decisive it makes me feel a tiny bit better. 'It's not that surprising, I suppose,' Kat goes on. 'Cassy loves babies. She's the right age. It's a wonder they waited this long, in fact.'

She's talking as if they *planned* it! Discussed it, even. Whereas my first thought is that it must be an *accident*, and that's why they've both been so stressed out recently.

'Dad's too old to have a baby!' I protest. 'He's practically ancient. And why would he want one? He's got us.'

'Cassy will have won him round,' Kat says. 'How could he deny lovely Cassy her heart's desire? And men are never too old, anyway. It doesn't make any difference to them. They can have babies when they're pensioners!'

'But what about us?'

'We're grown-up! We're almost out of their hair. You'll be going to university soon. So they can start all over again, now, like a proper family.'

'Kat! Don't say that!'

'Why not? It's the truth, isn't it?' Her voice sounds bitter, and sad. 'Time you faced facts, Emily Woodman.'

Kat's still asleep, or pretending to be, when I get up next morning. Dad's making porridge and has left his stuff all over the table so there's nowhere for me to make my sandwiches for lunch. Cassy sips a cup of tea and looks white and sick and of course now I know why. I don't speak to either of them. Dad switches on the radio just as I'm leaving, and Kat screeches from the bedroom for him to shut up. It's a relief to get out of the caravan.

All morning I'm tense, waiting for Kat to text. I keep imagining the showdown with Cassy and Dad. If Kat hadn't guessed, how long would they have left it before they told us? It proves how embarrassed Dad is about the whole thing. But Cassy? Maybe she's just scared.

Kat finally texts me after lunch, in Photography. I'm in the darkroom, so I have to wait till the end of the lesson to read it.

'What's up?' Rachel and I are walking down to town at the end of school. 'Did Mr Ives say something weird again?'

'I got a message from Kat,' I say.

'And?'

'Cassy's having a baby.'

Reading the word *baby* makes it real. Saying the word out loud makes it even more so.

Rachel stops to hug me. 'That's exciting! Aren't you pleased?'

'No.'

'Not even a teeny bit? Oh, Em, a little baby sister! Cassy will be a lovely mum. It'll be so cute.' She's almost skipping along, ridiculously happy.

106

I just want to cry.

'Don't be so grumpy about it, Em. When's it due?'

'June, Kat says.'

'A summer baby, like you. So you'll have moved into your huge house by then. You'll have so much space you'll hardly notice a baby.'

'How can you say that? It will change everything! Just imagine if your dad was having a new baby with that woman he's going out with –'

'I know. I think I'd be pleased. For them, and for me.'

'Well, maybe that's because you're living with your mum. And you don't already have a sister. You wouldn't feel like you were being pushed out.'

'Your dad's not pushing you out, Em!'

'Isn't he? That's what it feels like. It's like a slap in the face. We're not enough, me and Kat. They want their own proper family, him and Cassy.'

We have to shut up, then, because we've reached the market stall and Polly's waiting impatiently because we're a bit late.

'Thank goodness!' she says. 'It's been hectic all day. They've been here in coachloads. I need to go and fetch some new stock.'

We sort ourselves out. We put on our scarves and necklaces. But my heart's not in it any more. All I can think of is the stupid baby.

'Shall I get us something to eat?' Rachel says. 'We forgot, on the way here. I'm starving!'

I watch her disappear through the crowds. It's dusk already: a grey gloom that even the fairy lights don't seem to lift. The market stalls look tatty and dull instead of magical and Christmassy.

I sell one scarf, one stripy basket and a pair of silver snowflake earrings. The coachloads have gone home. It's quieter than it has been all week. I get out my phone. One message, from Seb. My heart lifts as I read it:

Pick you up after work? Got Mum's car for the evening. xx S

YES! I text back. *Thank you! xx E*

Rachel comes back with two hot cheese pasties and two cups of spiced apple. 'There! That'll cheer you up.'

'Seb's going to meet me after work,' I say. 'You can meet him.'

'At last! How's it going with you two?'

'OK,' I say. 'I thought he might be a bit fed up with me. Something I said last time. But he wants to go out tonight, so that's good.'

'I don't know why you're so secretive about him.'

'I don't know either.'

'You keep things to yourself. You always have done. But you like him a lot, don't you?'

'Yes.'

We have to stop talking to serve a customer. Polly is very insistent about it: not to keep chatting while we're serving. We're supposed to pay attention to the customer instead. Be nice to them. You sell more that way.

'How's Luke?' I ask Rachel, once the woman has moved off.

Rachel shrugs. 'OK. Ish. He's always busy, though. With the band and everything. Practising, or doing gigs. Or seeing his mates.'

'At least you get to see him at school.'

Polly turns up again with an armload of boxes. She plonks them down on a chair. 'There you are! You can unpack that lot while it's quiet. Put some more earrings on display too. The seasonal ones are selling best. Snowflakes, stars and the little silver Christmas trees. Everything OK, girls?' She's off again before we've even answered.

'She's always in a rush,' I say.

'Can you imagine doing what she does, all day? A scarf shop! Honestly!'

'Don't suppose she planned it. You wouldn't think, now what shall I do when I grow up? Oh yes: sell scarves.'

'Yeah. She'll have drifted into it. Like Mum and the video shop.'

'What did she do before?'

'Before what? Before Dad left? She stopped work when she had me. Before that, she was a PA for some businessman. But Dad started earning so much, she didn't need to work. Now look. He's got loads of money and a huge house, and she has practically nothing.'

'Your dad works ridiculously long hours, though,' I say. 'And he never seems happy, really, does he?'

Rachel doesn't answer. She's watching a group of homeless blokes ambling along between the stalls in the row next to ours. 'What happened to that bloke who had the heart attack?'

'Bob? He's still in hospital,' I say. She already knows about Mattie.

* * *

'There he is! In the black coat and jeans, with the brown hair.'

We watch Seb navigate his way to our stall. I'm dead proud of how lovely he looks.

Rachel starts smiling. She twiddles her hair like she used to do when we sat next to each other in Year Seven.

'Hey,' Seb says. 'Hello, Em. You look – a bit different!'

I laugh. 'Bit more colourful?' I unwrap the orange silk scarf. 'This is Rachel,' I say.

'Hello, Seb! Emily's told me all about you.'

His ears go red. Then he recovers and says hi to Rach. 'When do you finish?' he asks me.

'About ten minutes,' I say.

'You can go now, if you want,' Rachel says. 'I'll close up the stall and everything. It's fine.'

'Thanks!' I hug her.

'He's gorgeous!' she whispers in my ear. 'You jammy thing!'

'I haven't really told Rachel all about you,' I say as soon as we're out of earshot.

'No. I know that. You're a secretive person.'

'Am I? That's what Rachel just said. Weird.'

'Must be true, then. Anyway, it's fine. I'm like that too.'

We turn down Green Street to the cafe on the corner. We choose a table at the window and sit down.

I'm exhausted, suddenly.

When the waitress brings our coffees over, she only looks at and speaks to Seb. She watches him from behind the counter. Seb doesn't notice.

'What's the matter?' he says to me.

'Nothing. Just tired.'

'There's something else. I can tell.'

'Secrets,' I say. 'I'm sick of them.'

We sip our coffees. Seb reaches across for my hand and keeps hold of it, and for some reason that makes my eyes fill with tears.

I tell him about Dad's baby. 'That's one secret that isn't a secret any more.'

He doesn't say anything for a while. He just holds my hand.

It's nearly seven o'clock, and I know I should've phoned home to say I'm going to be late. Dad and Cassy will be expecting me back any minute. But I don't phone. Let them worry. They deserve it.

We finish our coffees.

'Did your sister get back OK?' Seb asks.

'Yes. Last night. But she's in a funny mood and the caravan's too small for four and we're all getting on each other's nerves.'

'Shall we go somewhere else, then?' Seb says. He leans forward and kisses me. 'If you could choose to be anywhere, in the whole world, where would you choose?'

'I don't know. An island, somewhere hot?'

It starts as a game. We take turns, thinking of places.

'The Outer Hebrides, in an unusually hot sunny summer, on a beach of white sand.'

'Antarctica. The last wilderness.'

'Under the sea. That's supposed to be the last wilderness, isn't it?'

'Actually,' I say, 'where I'd really like to be is in the middle of a wood, away from any houses or people. Surrounded by really old trees all covered in silvery lichen. And it's just starting to snow.'

Seb glances at the window, as if he thinks I mean it really is snowing.

I laugh. 'I'm just imagining it,' I say. 'We're in this wood, and the first flakes are spinning down from the leaden sky. Soon everything will be covered in a carpet of white, and a deep silence will descend, all except for the sound of snow sliding down branches, a sort of shushing sound.'

'You're bonkers!' Seb leans across the table and kisses me. 'Lyrical, but crazy.'

He tastes of coffee. And cinnamon.

'The best writers are,' I say. 'Like Blake. Or Emily Dickinson.'

'I didn't know you wanted to be a writer,' Seb says. 'I thought you were a photographer.'

'Why do I have to be just one thing?' I say.

We're both quiet, walking back across town to the place Seb's parked the car, near the children's play area. We go past the edge of the boating pond, where the ducks are sleeping with their heads tucked tight into their feathery backs. We pass the swings and the roundabout and the skate park. It's eerie, with no one there. We take a short cut across the grass. It's stiff with frost. Somewhere, a dog barks.

'I wish we had Mattie with us,' I say.

'We could go and see her.'

'What, now? It'll be all locked up!'

'We could go and look over the wall. See her in her pen. If she's in a pen?'

'They'll have guard dogs!'

'What, stray ones? German shepherd rescue dogs.'

'Rottweilers, probably. Or Staffordshire bull terriers.'

'Scary.'

'I'd rather go in the daytime. We could take Mattie out for a walk.'

'We could kidnap her. Steal her away and hide her somewhere.'

'Dognap.'

'What?'

'Not kidnap: dognap.'

'Oh. Dognap sounds like a kind of sleep.'

'That's catnap.'

'A dognap would be noisier. More smelly. Lots of grunting and snoring and dreaming.'

'Mattie used to dream. Her legs would kick out, and her ears twitch, and she'd make little whimpering noises.'

'We'll go after school one day, shall we? Or at the weekend? Unless you're still working.'

'We finish on Friday.'

'Saturday, then?'

We wipe the thin film of ice from the windscreen. Seb draws my initials in the frost.

'I thought I might have upset you, last time,' I say.

'No. Well, you did, but you were right.'

'Really?'

'Come here, you.'

He kisses me under the orange street light. When I close my eyes, I see orange stars.

'You could at least have phoned,' Dad says the minute I walk through the door. 'You knew we'd be worried.'

'Sorry.'

'Where've you been all this time?'

'School, work, then a cafe. Then I had to get back here, which is miles and takes ages, Dad. As you know. Anyway, where's everyone else?'

'Kat's at a friend's house, and Cassy's in the shower.'

'Which friend?'

'Mara. Her and lots of her old school friends. Tea?'

'Yes, please.'

'Did that boy give you a lift home?'

'Yes. So?'

Dad doesn't answer. He fills the kettle and then he makes me a sandwich, without me even asking. He drops the knife and fumbles about as if he's nervous. He puts the plate and my tea next to me on the sofa. Finally he clears his throat.

'Em, there's something I want to tell you.'

'Don't bother,' I say. 'I already know.'

Dad stares at the telly, which isn't even on.

'You and Cassy are having a baby.' I say it in a silly sing-song voice.

He looks hurt. I don't care.

'Did Kat tell you?'

'Yes.'

'She was supposed to wait.'

'Well, she didn't. What difference does it make?'

'Are you – what – I mean . . .'

'What?'

'Cassy is very happy. WE are very happy,' Dad says.

'That's all right, then.'

'You're not making this very easy,' Dad says. 'Don't be like this, Em.'

'Like what?'

'Cross and unhelpful.'

'What did you expect?'

'I thought you might be pleased. Excited, even. Happy for me and Cassy.'

'You thought wrong, then.'

It's too late to take the words back. Later, when Cassy comes back from her shower, I hear their low voices, urgent and anxious, whispering to each other. I feel bad for hurting Dad. A bit bad, anyway.

I peer out of the oblong slit of window into the darkness. I think for a moment about Bob, stuck in his isolation room, in the hospital with its windows all lit up like a ferry sailing into the night. I imagine Mattie curled in a corner of her horrible pen in the dogs' home, alone and afraid. I wait for Seb to send me

a goodnight text. I wait and wait. Finally I send one
to him, instead, and he answers straight away.

Thinking of you. Love you.

I stare at it for a long, long time.

13

Seb meets me at the top of the lane on Saturday afternoon. I climb in the car and lean over to kiss him.

'Mmm. You smell nice,' he says. 'Your hair.'

'Cassy's drawn us a map of how to get there,' I say. I spread it out on my lap.

'You two are speaking again, then.'

'Yes. It's all calmed down a bit. Kat's been staying over at Mara's. I've been making an effort to be nice.'

The reception area at the dogs' home is crowded with people. Seb can hardly believe his eyes. This is all new to him. 'A queue? To take a mangy dog for a walk?'

'Got some identity?' the woman at the desk asks me. I show her my school student card, to prove I'm me, and over sixteen.

She prints me off a name tag, and puts it into a plastic cover.

'Clip that on your coat,' she says, 'then join the queue.'

'It's like a top security prison!' Seb says. 'Ridiculous! They're stray dogs, for heaven's sake!'

'Shh! We'll lose our licence if we mess about.'

It's our turn. A girl leads us through a door to the dog cages outside. There's a terrible din of barking dogs and the smell is disgusting.

Mattie's ears prick up when she sees me. She stands up, legs trembling. She looks even thinner than before.

'Hey, Mattie!' I call. 'It's me.'

'You must keep her on the lead the whole time,' the girl says. 'And take a bag for any dog mess. You must clear it up and put it in the bins near the gate.'

Seb grins at me. 'That'll be your job.'

The girl clips the lead on to Mattie's collar and hands it to me. 'She's very good, this one. Sweet-natured. She doesn't pull.'

'I know,' I say.

People with dogs straining at the leash are heading off over the field next to the home, so Seb and me go the other way. On the other side of the road we find a stile, and a footpath sign, so we head down there. Mattie doesn't want to climb the stile, so we lift her over between us. Her heart beats fast and hot against my hand.

'She's scared, poor thing.'

'She's too thin. She's pining for Bob.'

'We should have brought her something to eat.'

Mattie's the kind of dog that needs to run and run. It's cruel to keep her on the end of a short lead. So, once we're well away from the road we unclip her. She trots between us. Her confidence comes back after a while and she runs ahead. She keeps coming back, though, as if to check we're still with her. We stroke her head and she nuzzles my hand with her nose.

The path goes along next to a stone wall, and then there's another stile, and we're at the edge of woodland. A sign says: *National Trust. No fires, no overnight camping. Please take your litter home.* The path gets muddier, and overgrown with brambles, but we keep going and after a bit it opens out and we're in a proper old wood, with thick, twisted vines hanging down from the bare-boned trees, and ivy and all sorts. The ground is marshy and damp underfoot. Mattie runs and barks and then skitters around, chasing imaginary rabbits into the undergrowth, burrowing and digging and making the piles of old leaves flurry and fly up. She disappears for a while and I start to worry.

'Let's follow where she went,' I say.

Under the bigger trees the ground is much drier.

'Beech and oak and hazel, mostly,' Seb says. 'Mixed deciduous woodland.'

I pull a face. 'Show-off.'

He grabs me and wrestles me to the ground. We stay there, lying together on the piles of damp leaves, and stare up at the patches of sky between the bare branches. In the west it's turning a pinky orange as the sun goes down.

'If something happened to all the human beings,' Seb says, 'in a very short time, England would be covered in trees again, like it used to be. One huge forest.'

'You say that as if it would be good,' I say.

'I like thinking about it,' Seb says. 'That we're not very important, really. If we mess up the world, it will

119

just recover. Nature will, I mean. There just won't be any people to see it.'

'So global warming and climate change doesn't matter?'

'Of course it matters! It will mean horrible things for millions of people. But the planet will adapt and recover. The earth will go on living.'

I think about that.

Seb rolls over and puts his face against mine. 'You're cold,' he says.

'Better warm me up, then.'

He holds me tight. His hair tickles my face. He traces the line of my lips with his finger.

'You realise we've found a wood for you,' Seb says. 'Now all we need is snow.'

'The sky's too clear. It's not cold enough. It's probably never going to snow again in England!'

'Can you remember it properly snowing, ever? When you were little?'

'Once, maybe. I used to love stories where it snowed.'

'*Narnia*.'

'Yes. And *The Snow Queen*. Kat read that to me. It was in this book . . . one our mother left behind.'

'Your real mother.'

'Yes. Francesca.'

'What happened to her?'

'She ran away. I don't really know what happened, exactly. Just what Kat told me, when we were little. Dad used to get too upset when we asked about her. So we stopped asking questions.'

'How old were you, when she left?'

'I was two. Kat was four.'

'Where is she now?'

'No idea.'

'She doesn't write, or phone, or anything?'

'Nothing. Never has.'

Seb thinks about that for a while. 'We should find her. Track her down.'

'That's what Rachel says. Kat's dead against it. I've looked her name up before, but I didn't find anyone that might be her.'

Mattie comes snuffling up. We've almost forgotten about her. She curls up close to me and Seb, and the three of us lie there for a little longer, just resting and being close, like it's a comfort to all three of us.

I get my camera out to take some photographs. The bare bones of the tree branches against the sunset sky. Mattie curled up next to Seb: the texture of her wiry fur against Seb's woollen coat, close-up. Seb stretching his arms out, lying on a bed of leaves.

Taking photographs helps me to see things properly, and to remember them. I know we'll come back here. In the summer it will be beautiful: sheltered and private under a thick canopy of leaves. It can be our special place. If we're still together, that is, Seb and me.

I like to think we will be.

I haven't ever felt like this about anyone before.

It's getting dark. As the light goes, the temperature drops too. My hands and toes are freezing. I put the camera back in my bag.

'Come on, then,' I say. I haul Seb up. 'Home time, Mattie.'

We follow her to begin with, thinking she'll lead us back to the path. She does, except after a while we work out it's a different footpath and we seem to be going downhill, instead of up. We stop to get our bearings, but we can't see anything much now it's dark.

'We're lost,' Seb says.

'The footpath must go somewhere. Let's just follow it up the hill.'

It twists and turns and we're about to stop again and rethink when we stumble across a stretch of stone wall.

'There was a wall like this before,' Seb says. 'Near that stile, where we started off. Let's follow it along.'

I'm beginning to feel weary. We've walked miles. My feet are wet through even in boots. Seb holds my hand, and Mattie trots behind. Eventually we come to a cluster of stone buildings. Some sort of farm. A cobbled courtyard. A stone archway, and beyond it, a street light. But first there's a high wire fence, and a field with dark shapes in it.

'If we can climb through,' Seb says, 'we can cut across to the road.'

The air smells different. It takes me a while to work out what the smell is. Pine. The dark shapes in the field are trees. It's a nursery of trees: rows of them. We find a bit of fence where we can pull the wire apart enough to climb through. Mattie won't come: she starts to whine.

'I'll pick her up,' Seb says, 'and you hold the wires. There might be farm dogs or something. We don't want her to bark.'

We walk along the grass strips between the rows of trees. The pine smell is even stronger. The wind catches the pine needles and makes a whispering sound.

'It's a Christmas tree farm,' Seb says. 'Big business.'

'I know where we are, then,' I say. 'It's on Cassy's map. Rainbow Wood Farm. We've come round in a big circle.'

'We could take a tree back with us.'

'That would be stealing!'

'Just a tiny one that no one would miss?'

'Better to leave them alive and growing.'

'But they'll cut them all, eventually. It's just a cash crop. Like cut flowers.'

'Except, it takes a tree years to grow. And a tree has a soul.'

'A what?'

'A soul. I know, you think that's rubbish. Irrational nonsense. But it's what I feel. So shut up.'

Seb laughs. 'I never said a word.'

We've reached the other side of the field, and the edge of the courtyard. 'Imagine coming up here and decorating all the little trees, in the field, while they are growing,' I say. 'That would be cool.'

Seb gives me that look, like I've gone totally bananas now.

'It would be a good photograph,' I say. 'Imagine!'

Mattie stops, nose quivering, ears forward as if she's heard something. Seb grabs my arm. 'Shall we run for it?' he says. 'Across the courtyard, out on to the road, before anyone sees us?'

I'm giggling too much to run fast. Seb half drags me, and Mattie starts to bark, but we're through the stone arch and on to the tarmac road before the barn door swings wide open and someone shouts out. We really run then.

The girl at the dogs' home is cross with us for being so late back with Mattie.

'She's all cold and wet, too!' she says.

'She loved her walk,' I say back. 'And it's much nicer for her than being shut in a wire cage all afternoon.'

It's like I'm betraying Mattie, handing her over again to be locked up.

'We'll take her out again,' Seb says as we cross the car park. 'It was fun. Even getting lost was fun.'

'What will you be doing for Christmas Day?' he asks me when we're driving home. 'You could come to our house, if you like. Mum said. Meet the cousins and my aunties.'

'Dad wouldn't allow me. We have to be a family all together. We're going out for the day as a treat. Cassy refuses to cook Christmas dinner in a caravan.'

'I've got you a present,' Seb says. 'You could come over in the evening? Just for a little while? I'll collect you.'

I smile, thinking about him, all the way down the lane and across the field to the caravan. It's changed everything for me, meeting Seb.

Dad's car isn't there, but the lights are on in the caravan.

Kat's home.

She's lolling on the sofa in front of the telly.

'Where's Dad and Cass?'

'Out with friends. A party or something.'

'Are you going to be staying in?'

'Yes. You?'

'Yes.'

We have the best evening. We make pasta and sauce and eat it in front of rubbish telly, and we talk about Dan, and I tell her a bit about Seb.

'Have you slept with him?' she asks.

I blush. 'No,' I say. 'In any case, it's none of your business.'

'Just be careful, that's all,' Kat says. 'You know about contraception and everything, don't you?'

'Of course.'

'And don't be in a hurry. It's better if you wait. Like, be sure he's the right person, really special.'

'I know all that,' I say. 'Why are you telling me?' I look at Kat's face. Her eyes are brimming with tears.

'I wish I'd waited,' Kat says. 'I wish my first time had been really special. I wish I'd waited for Dan.'

'Oh, Kat!' I hug her.

'He phoned today. I'm going up there on Boxing Day,' she says.

I make a sad face. 'You've hardly been here and you're off again!'

'That's life!' She grins. 'You'll survive! Anyway, you've got Seb, now.'

'What can I give him for Christmas? He just told me he's got me a present.'

'What is it?'

'He didn't tell me that, stupid! It's a secret.'

'You should give him something special, not something you just go and buy. Make him something. I don't know, a cake? Sew him something?'

'I can't sew!'

'A photograph, then. Give him one of your lovely photos. A black and white one, in a frame.'

We look at all the photos in my scrapbook, and then start going through all the hundreds of digital ones on the computer.

Kat gets bored after a while. 'You choose,' she says. 'You don't need me to help. It's a good idea, though, isn't it?'

'Yes. You are brilliant. My best, most favourite sister in the world.'

'Your only sister,' she starts to say, only she stops, suddenly, and looks at me. 'Oh my God.' Her hand goes to her mouth. 'You know what I'm thinking?'

'Yes.'

In six months' time. A new sister.

'It might be a boy, of course,' she says.

'Would that be better or worse?'

'Worse. Can't you imagine? Dad, with a boy? The only son and heir. All that.'

'He wouldn't be like that.'

'No?'

'Cassy wouldn't let him,' I say.

'Anyway, I won't be around to see. I'm going to make sure of that.'

14

I'm waiting for him in the lay-by, at four in the afternoon, the earliest we can each get away from our families.

'Hop in!' Seb says.

He puts his arm round me. I breathe in the warm smell of his hair, his skin.

'Happy Chr—' I'm about to say, but Seb puts his finger on my lips. 'Wait,' he says. 'Save it for when we get there.'

'Where?'

'Wait and see.'

I sit with his present on my lap, all beautifully wrapped up in layers of blue coloured tissue with little gold stars between each layer, and thin gold silk ribbon tied round in a bow.

He doesn't drive us to his house, like I expected. He goes left, towards town, and then up the hill towards the dogs' home, and for a second my heart feels heavy, because I can't bear to see Mattie's sad face today. But he drives past the entrance, and parks a little bit down the road, not far from Rainbow Wood Farm.

'Will you be warm enough?' Seb asks. 'I brought an

extra scarf in case.' He rummages around on the back seat and lugs out a bag full of stuff. 'Stop looking. It's got to be a surprise.'

The air hits us: frost-cold. It's madness to set out on walk at this time of day, in the middle of winter. We climb over the stile and go down the same footpath we took before.

Seb stops in front of me. His breath makes smoke clouds in the frosty air. 'Now close your eyes,' he orders me. 'Keep them tight shut. Promise?' He takes my hand and leads me off the path. I've already guessed where we're going, but I don't say.

My feet trip and stumble on unseen bits of log and twigs and uneven ground. I start to laugh.

'Don't open your eyes yet!' He ties the spare scarf round my face, so I can't cheat. 'Now stand still. Wait there.'

His footsteps crunch over dead leaves, gradually getting further away. It's odd, standing alone and blindfolded like that. Little by little, I hear other sounds: my own breathing, and a bird scratching about; a rook or crow caws from high in some tree. Closer, a smaller bird makes a *chit-chit-chit* sound.

'Hear that? It's a wren.'

Seb's voice startles me. I haven't heard him creeping back.

'Now walk forward again, about twenty steps, straight ahead, then stop.'

I count the twenty steps and wait.

He unwinds the scarf. 'Now look!'

Just in front of me in the centre of the clearing in the trees stands a tiny real Christmas tree in a pot. He's decorated it with angel-hair and tiny glass baubles, all different colours, and instead of a star at the top there is a heart, stitched out of white felt with a heart-shaped mirror in the middle. Underneath the tree is a brown parcel tied up with string.

'It's magical,' I say. I can hardly believe Seb has done all this for me.

'Because you like trees,' Seb says. 'Your own special tree that's still growing, in its pot, so you can plant it somewhere if you want. A wood or your garden at the new house or whatever.'

I put my present for Seb under the little tree. He takes a box of matches out of his pocket and tries to light the candles – real ones, like birthday-cake candles, which he's fixed with fine wire on to the pine-needle branches – but they keep going out. We sit close together on the fallen log, and wrap the scarf round us, but it's still freezing cold.

'We should light a fire,' Seb says.

'Someone will see. Come and tell us off.'

'Like who? No one will be around today!'

So we gather bits of fallen branch and twigs and pile it all up, and Seb gets it to light by lying down and blowing at it, from beneath, and fanning the tiny flame. And I think, this is the most perfect Christmas ever, Seb and me together like this.

'Happy Christmas, Emily Woodman,' Seb says, reaching for the parcel under the little tree.

'It feels like a book,' I say. I untie the string.

·'For your photographs,' Seb says, 'or for writing in. Or for both!'

The cover is blue and gold, and the endpapers are marbled, and the paper inside is blue, hand-made paper with bits of petal and flecks of gold thread woven into the paper itself.

'It's beautiful. Almost too beautiful to use!'

Seb unwraps his framed photographs from me. One is of Mattie, in black and white, and the other is the river, and a figure running. He peers at it.

'Is it me?'

'Yes!'

'They're good, Em. Really good. Thank you!'

He kisses me. We hold each other tight. We kiss some more.

The fire splutters and falters, the green wood hissing and spitting.

Frost sparkles on the dry leaves at our feet. The air smells of smoke, and ice.

'Your nose is freezing!'

It's hard to leave this magical place, but we're both cold to the bone.

'Come on, then,' I say at last. 'Let's go back to your house. Just for a short time.'

We stamp out the last embers of the fire. Seb puts everything back into his bag. We carry the little tree between us.

We go back to join his family party, drinking home-made beer, and eating Christmas cake with thick white icing. His aunties and cousins are all there. We play silly games like charades, and for once I don't mind too much.

Seb's mum's had too much to drink. She talks too fast, too much, her eyes all shiny and big. She sits on the arm of the chair next to me and leans into me. 'He's a changed boy,' she says. 'You've worked a little magic on him, Emmy darling. I knew all he needed was the love of a good woman!'

Seb comes over to rescue me. 'Em's got to get back soon,' he tells her. 'I need to take her home.'

We go via Moat House, to find a place for my tree. We leave it at the edge of the copse near the river, still with its baubles and candles. I put the heart in my pocket, to take home with me.

'We're going to Auntie Ruby's for New Year. I can't get out of it,' Seb says when he drops me off at the lay-by. 'I'll see you when we get back, yes?'

I hug him tight.

'Love you,' Seb says.

'Love you,' I say.

I put the felt heart under my pillow at bedtime. I smooth the empty pages of my new photograph-and-writing book. I start thinking about all the words that will fill it up, all the things that haven't happened yet. My heart is full. It's like I'm on the edge of something extraordinary, and I can hardly wait for it all to unfold.

Notebook 2 Blue and Gold
January to March

1

I'm sitting in the caravan, watching the rain slide down the windows. So far, it has rained every day since Boxing Day. The river at Moat House is swollen, a brown swirling torrent right up to the top of the banks, and Dad's started worrying it'll flood the house itself. But the house has stood there long enough, Cassy says. 'Things are changing, though,' Dad says. 'The world's changing fast, and the patterns of the weather are changing too. It never used to rain like this.'

The building work's ground to a halt what with Christmas and New Year holidays and the rain. This week, Dad's been going down there to try and get things moving again. We are all getting on each other's nerves, cooped up in this stupid caravan in the middle of a sodden field. Kat's still in London.

I check my emails for the millionth time. Nothing new. No texts from Seb, either. I can't understand it.

'Shall we do something, you and me?' Cassy asks. 'You're so fed up.'

'Like what?'

'We could go shopping . . . the sales are on. Or go to

see a film? What would you like?'

'Nothing, really. It's raining too much to go anywhere.'

'We could go and see Bob, at the hospital. I know it's not much of an outing. But I haven't been for ages. We need to see how he is, tell him about Mattie. We could take him something.'

'Such as?'

'I don't know. Something to eat? Hospital food is rubbish these days. What does he like?'

'Cheap cider. Chips.'

Cassy laughs. 'OK, then, let's get him fish and chips on the way in.'

'The nurses won't allow us, Cassy.'

'We'll say they're for us. We can secretly feed chips to Bob, when they're not looking.'

'Is he better enough to eat chips?'

'I don't know. We'll find out, won't we? Last time, they wouldn't even let me see him. I should've been back before, but what with Christmas and everything . . .'

Cassy's driving's worse than Seb's, even though she passed her test years ago. We have to have the windows open and no radio or music on because she says she gets distracted and doolally. Having a baby is making her even more like that, she says. She doesn't like reversing, so we search for a huge parking space. Even so, she swears a lot and huffs and puffs, going backwards and forwards. 'Sorry about the language,' she says.

'I don't mind,' I say. 'I've heard much worse.'

'You should get Seb to teach you to drive,' Cassy says once she's got the car straightened up. She's gone over the white lines on one side. 'I'd be useless at teaching you.'

I laugh. She's right; she would.

'You haven't seen him for a while. You haven't fallen out with him, have you?'

'No. He's at his auntie's. On some island that isn't an island any more, in Dorset. But he's back tomorrow, I think.'

'Such a lovely boy,' Cassy says. 'You fell on your feet there.'

Cassy does a quick dash to the loo while I get the parking ticket. It's still drizzling. Maybe it's a good thing Bob's warm and dry in hospital, instead of out on the streets in the endless rain. We've forgotten about the chips, I realise. Just as well. Cassy's a bit mad sometimes.

I follow her through the swing doors and along a corridor and up two flights of stairs. Cassy stops at the nurses' station to ask for Bob. Three of them in dark blue uniforms are having a laugh about something, but they sober up when Cassy mentions Bob's name.

'Mr Bob Moss,' Cassy says again.

'Are you a relative?' The nurse in charge frowns at us like we're bad news or something.

'Just friends,' Cassy says. 'Bob doesn't have any relatives, as far as we know. Is there a problem?'

One of the nurses *click-clacks* away down the corridor, and the other one starts flicking through the pages in the big diary on the desk.

Our nurse stands up. 'I'm sorry,' she says. 'Could you come through into the office, for a moment?' She looks at me. 'Perhaps your daughter could stay here.'

'I'm not her daughter,' I start saying, but she's already shutting the door behind her and Cassy. So I wander off down the corridor. The ward stinks: boiled cabbage and poo. I walk past a row of single rooms with notices on the doors: *No unauthorised entry. High Infection Risk.* I've got a bad feeling about it all even before Cassy calls me. Her voice is teary and her hair's all mussed up.

'I'm so sorry, Em. I should've left a number with the ward manager. I should've called her before. I feel terrible we didn't know.'

'What's happened? Cassy? Tell me.'

She's crying so much it's hard to take in what she's saying, even though I kind of know instantly what she's about to say.

'Bob isn't here. Bob died just before Christmas.'

He caught an infection and he was too weak and unfit to fight it off. His liver packed up. That, and the heart attack that started it all off.

'All this time and we didn't know,' Cassy keeps saying, as if that's the worst thing. 'All through Christmas and everything.'

She's so upset it means I can't be. That's the way it seems to work, like only one person at a time can be really sad. So I hand her tissues and give her hugs and she cries quietly all the way back to the car park.

Back in the car, I suddenly think: *Mattie! What now?*

'It was supposed to cheer us up,' Cassy says mournfully. 'Our trip out for the day. Now look at us.' She sniffs.

'Let's go and get fish and chips, anyway,' I say. 'Let's remember nice things about Bob, you and me. And then we have to think what to do about Mattie.'

Cassy blows her nose like a great trumpet. 'Thanks, darling,' she says. 'You're so grown-up and sensible these days. I'm sorry I'm like this. It's those hormones running riot. I can't help it.'

'Are you OK to drive?'

Cassy nods. 'We'll go to the Jazz Cafe and have a slap-up lunch and take it from there.'

So that's what we do.

We talk about what should happen to Mattie. I think we should go and get her straight away, look after her ourselves. It's horrible to think of her in that place, all unloved and lonely.

'I'll do everything,' I say. 'I'll feed her and take her for walks every day. Once we're all in the big house, it won't be a problem.'

'But you're at school all day. And you're not always going to be around, are you? You'll be off like Kat at the end of next year. And then there's the baby coming . . . We've got to think sensibly, Em, long-term.'

'Long-term there'll be masses of space. The garden's so big she won't even need taking for walks;

she can just run in the fields. Moat House is huge. And it will be nice for the stupid baby. I think you're being selfish and mean.'

'Emily!' Cassy sounds genuinely shocked. But she doesn't start crying again. She goes silent, which is almost worse.

It's like she's actually counting down the days till both Kat and me will be gone. It's horrible, realising that. They've got it all planned out, Cassy and Dad.

Life after us.

2

Seb phones me as soon as they get back from his auntie's house on Portland. I tell him about Bob straight away.

'He wasn't even old,' I say. 'He looked it because of being out in all weathers. But he was only about thirty. And Cassy won't let us have Mattie. All she cares about is herself and Dad and the baby. She never thinks about what I might want. It's like I just don't matter any more.'

'Shall I come and get you?' Seb asks. 'I've got the car. You can come back to my house for the evening.'

Almost as soon as I've got in the car I start crying. I feel such a twit. But just the way Seb looks at me, and puts his arms round me makes it all come flooding out.

'Sorry,' I say, once I've got myself sorted a bit. 'It's all got too much. It's that stupid caravan driving me crazy. There's nowhere to escape.'

Seb tells me about Portland while he drives us back to his house. I haven't seen him so animated about anything before. There's some stone quarry place, apparently, where you can learn how to do proper carving and lettering and things. You can get qualifications in it, even. 'I might do the course,' he says. 'If I can get the money for it, somehow. Portland stone is famous. St Paul's Cathedral's made of it. Lots of other famous buildings too. It's a unique kind of limestone, but much harder and longer lasting than other kinds. You get a really clean line. Sharp. And the stone has this amazing way of both absorbing and reflecting light. When the sun shines, it's luminous. Dazzling.'

Upstairs in his room, he shows me more stuff on the computer about the limestone beds in the quarries. 'When this was all formed, the sea was warm, like the Bahamas today. There are loads of fossils in the stone. Ammonites and other creatures. Insects that died when they fell into the salty water in the lagoons. And there are bits of forest too. A kind of cypress tree that's extinct now.

'Imagine,' he says. 'You can split open a face of stone that has been hidden since it was formed a million years ago, and be the first person to see it. That's awesome!'

'You'd have to go and live down there,' I say, 'if you wanted to do the course. It's too far to travel from here.'

'Yeah. I can stay at my Auntie Ruby's. She's already said I can.'

We lie on his bed together. I kick off my shoes. It begins to dawn on me that this is why Seb didn't phone all the time he was away. He's totally taken up with this new project. It's a side of Seb I haven't seen before.

'I can feel your heart beating,' Seb says. 'Ever so fast!' He keeps his hand there.

I slip my hand under his T-shirt, on to his warm chest.

'. . . *two hearts beating each to each.*'

Seb looks at me. 'You what?'

'It's from a poem,' I say. 'Robert Browning. It just popped into my head. It starts with the *grey sea*, and the *long black land*, and a *yellow half-moon large and low* . . . and two lovers meeting.'

We kiss. He traces my lips with his fingers, and kisses me again, harder. My body melts under his touch. The kissing and the touching make everything else go away. Nothing matters so much any more.

It's enough for me, just lying together so close, like this. I think about what Kat said to me, when we were talking together before Christmas. I'm not ready for anything more than touching and kissing, not yet. But Seb is. I know that, even though he hasn't said so, exactly.

The front door bangs. 'Your mum's back,' I say.

Seb goes out to the loo.

I go slowly downstairs. 'Hello, Avril.'

She gives me a big hug. 'Are you all right, love? You look a bit *fragile.*'

I tell her about Bob while she puts on the kettle and unpacks her shopping.

'I heard about the baby too,' Avril says. 'I expect things are a bit hard for you all in that tiny caravan.

You can come here whenever you want some breathing space, you know.'

'Thank you,' I say.

'Can you stay for tea tonight?'

I nod.

'He missed you, that week away,' Avril says. 'He might not tell you that, but I can read him like a book.'

I smile.

'And the cousins were all asking about you. You made quite an impression. Ruby calls you the princess.'

I don't know what to say to that.

'Seb's her special favourite,' Avril says. 'Of all the nephews.'

'He might be going to stay with her,' I say. 'To do that stone carving course.'

'Yes,' Avril says. 'Isn't it wonderful? He's found something he wants to do at last.'

She pours three mugs of tea. 'Take yours and Seb's upstairs to his room,' she says. 'Supper'll be ready in half an hour.'

Seb is sitting at the computer, clicking away at stuff.

'Come here,' he says. 'I want to show you something.'

I squeeze next to him on the chair.

'Look what I've found for you.'

It's so out of the blue, so not what I'm expecting. Maybe if we'd been talking about it before, or if he'd told me he'd been looking, I'd have been more prepared, more in control. It throws me completely. He's bookmarked pages of internet sites, all about tracing family members, reuniting families, that sort of thing. There are sites for information about missing persons, and maps and newspapers and records from all over the world. People who've run away from home; homeless people; sites for refugees and immigrants, adopted children . . . every variation of missing person you could possibly imagine and then more.

'I thought we could start looking for her. Your real mother.' He scrolls down some list and flicks from one site to another.

My head's already throbbing.

I start to feel sick.

'She's not a missing person,' I finally say. My mouth's dry.

'Well, not exactly. Missing from your life, though.'

'By choice. It was her decision.'

I know I sound weird. I've gone rigid and stony inside. I don't want to look at this stuff. I know he's spent ages finding it and everything but it's horrible. It's the wrong stuff. It doesn't help.

'She's got her own life somewhere. Just not with us,' I manage to say.

'But it wasn't your choice,' Seb says. He sounds slightly put out. 'You were only two years old. You've a right to know about her. She's your own mother.'

'Don't.'

'Don't what?'

'Stop it. Stop talking about it.'

'What's wrong with talking about it? It's important. We should be talking about it. We should be able to talk about everything, you and me.'

I can't speak. My hands are clammy.

'I'm trying to help,' Seb says. 'Show you there are ways we can find her. Together.'

'I don't think I want to.'

'What?'

I can hardly breathe. The walls of the room seem to loom in. The computer hum gets louder and louder. I stand up, dizzy, and stumble to the window. The sky's big and black; just a thin layer of grey cloud streaking above the horizon.

'I don't get it. You told me you'd started thinking about her. Wondering about her. Remember? When we were in the cafe. And then in the wood. It seemed really important, you telling me that. We can actually find her. Don't you see how big that is? How amazing it would be? All your questions . . . there would be answers for them. You don't have to do it by yourself. I'll help you.'

'Not like this.'

'Why not?'

'This is just horrible.'

'Why are you angry with me?'

I stare at the dark sky. I'm shaking with something – can't think – anger, or fear . . . I can't tell the difference any more.

'Come here,' Seb says. He holds his arm out as if to pull me in, closer.

I shrink away. 'You should have asked first. What I

wanted.' My words come out like bullets.

'I thought you'd be pleased. I did this for *you*. It took hours.'

My skin burns, then freezes. I'm shivering all over.

'You were wasting your time, then. You were just filling in the time, anyway, weren't you? Messing about on the stupid computer. You've got too much time doing nothing all day.' Even as I say the words I know how cruel and horrible they are. And not even true, any longer.

'For Christ's sake, Em. It's just a load of web pages. It's no big deal. You're overreacting big time.'

'If that's what you think, it shows how little you know. Or care.'

'That's not fair.'

'You haven't a clue about me, have you?'

'Now you're just being ridiculous. Childish.'

'Just shut up. Piss off. I don't need this.' I'm so furious I can't look at him. I storm into the loo and sit there with the door locked. My head's spinning as if I'm about to faint. And then I throw up.

Through the muddle and darkness inside, I begin to hear small sounds again. A tap, dripping. The whirr of the fan, and the click of the radiator turning on.

Feet pad along the landing. Voices drift upstairs from the kitchen.

I start to calm down.

What happens now?

I've gone too far.

Is this it? The end for me and Seb?

147

What should I do? It's too far to walk back home by myself. I could phone Cassy, who hates driving in the dark and is already in a mood with me. Dad's out tonight. I haven't any money for a taxi.

'Tea's ready,' Avril calls up from the kitchen.

I can hardly think. But how can I leave, now?

I rinse my face. I look terrible: my eyes red and swollen and piggy; my cheeks blotchy. I find a comb in the bathroom cupboard and sort my hair out.

Seb's already sitting at the table by the time I get downstairs. He doesn't even look up. All through the meal, Avril and Nick make polite conversation, and I answer their questions, and Seb doesn't say a word.

I carry dishes out to the kitchen. 'You hardly ate a thing,' Avril says.

'I need to go home, really,' I say. 'I'm tired. Thanks for dinner. It was really tasty. I'm sorry I didn't eat much.'

Seb's standing in the doorway, watching us.

'Well,' Avril says to him, 'you'd better take the princess home.'

Seb winces. 'Where are the car keys?'

'You had them last. Upstairs?'

'Did something happen to you two?' Avril asks me, while he's out of the room. 'You both seem miserable as sin.'

'I'm sorry,' I say. My eyes well up.

'You take care, Emily. Come again soon.' She gives me a peck on the cheek. 'Things have a way of working out. Don't you worry.'

* * *

148

Seb drives too fast. He glares at me when I suck in my breath as a lorry comes over the brow of the bridge and he has to brake sharply.

What should I say?

Not *sorry*. I'm not sorry. Why should I be? I didn't ask him to search out all that stuff. It's his fault I'm feeling like this.

But the silence is horrible.

It scares me, the way I can flip. I get trapped into another version of me, and then I can't find the way back out. It's happened before. It's as if being forced to think about finding Francesca has tipped me back in time, to being little, and helpless, all over again.

Seb hasn't seen this side of me before.

He pulls up at the top of the lane. 'There,' he says. Nothing else.

No kiss or hug.

'Bye,' I say, all frosty and mean.

Make the first move, the good Emily says in my head.

No. Why should I? The flip-side wins. I slam the car door.

He doesn't wait to watch me go down the lane. He spins the wheels as he turns the car, and speeds off.

I won't let myself cry. I walk down the lane to the gate, and across the field. It's too dark to see properly: I keep stepping into puddles in the deep ruts made by car wheels. I don't care.

I fumble for my keys. All the lights are off in the caravan. No one's home. I stumble in over the doorstep and fling myself down on the sofa. Still I don't cry.

I turn on my laptop. No one's on MSN. I try Facebook. Everyone's off-line. Everyone I know in the whole wide world is out somewhere having a good time. Bob's dead. I'm not allowed to have Mattie. Seb hates me.

I lie in the dark. I let myself sink down into it, this feeling of being utterly alone and abandoned.

Like a little child.

Like it's all over. Finished.

3

Sunlight streams through the classroom window, falling on to the table in squares of light, turning the piles of tissue and crêpe paper into glowing blocks of emerald green and stinging yellow.

Hold the thin sheet of tissue up to the light and it's like stained glass.

Cut out petal shapes, Mrs Levens says, and green spikes for the leaves. Stick them down on the card. Now you curl a strip of yellow crêpe round your finger and push the end, so it goes wavy. Glue down one end of the yellow tube, so it sticks out of the card to make the daffodil middle, like a trumpet. Our 3-D daffodil cards will make our mothers very happy. Now best writing, to go inside the card. No mistakes. Copy the letters from the whiteboard. Happy Mother's Day. *Now write a special message for your special mummy.*

I wander to the window sill. You are not supposed to get up and walk about in Class Five, but Mrs Levens doesn't notice because she's busy helping Tomas. I check on the tadpoles in the tank. They are just getting legs. We have given them a rock for climbing out on when they get four legs and that's when they have to breathe air. *My head is hot and my throat's gone tight. I want Kat and it's ages till playtime.*

'Come and sit down, please, Emily.'

Mrs Levens tugs my arm because I can't seem to move away from the window and the tadpoles. My legs don't want to move. The pondweed is a bit brown at the edges. Some tadpoles have two back legs and a tail. One is just a big fat tadpole and no legs at all. Sometimes that happens: they grow and grow but they don't change like they ought to.

Mrs Levens' jumper smells of washing powder. She crouches down next to me so she is the same height as me and she stays there while I write, Dear Cassy, Love from Emily. *We leave out the bit in the middle about mothers.*

4

I've gone over and over in my mind what Seb did and why it upset me so much. It was partly that I was already upset about Bob's death, and then, if I'm really honest, it was a bit hard to see Seb so excited about going away to do that course. But the real problem was the way he just took over, so I wasn't in control. Everything happened too fast.

The same thing happened when Rachel started going on about looking for my mum, back in the autumn.

It has to be my decision. I have to do it in my own time. If I do it at all, that is.

What if I do?

What would it be like, to find Francesca?

Since those few words Mr Ives said last October, it's been worming away at the back of my mind, the idea that I might actually be able to find her.

Something Rachel said keeps coming into my head: *I'd want to know the ways I was like her, and the ways I was different.*

It's beginning to make sense to me, now.

Finding my real mum might be part of finding me.

So now I'm starting to see (duh!) that's what Seb wanted to help me do. And that means I feel terrible about how I reacted. And terrified that I've blown it completely with him for ever.

His phone's still turned off.

I left a *sorry* message, earlier.

I tried phoning him again before school.

I've sent three texts. I can't send any more. So now what?

'What have you been up to today?' Cassy says when I get home from school. She's cooking a slap-up meal for Kat's return from London tonight with Dan. She's often in a chatty mood now she's started feeling so much better.

'Not much.'

'How's the Photography project?'

'OK,' I say. 'I can show you if you want.'

When she's got everything in the pan and has turned down the heat, she wipes her hands and sits down with me at the table.

Cassy looks thoughtful, flicking through the pages of my journal. She doesn't say much.

'I like this one.' She points at the photo of birch trunks making silvery shadows. 'It almost looks like a painting, instead of a photo,' Cassy says. 'How do you do that, then?'

I explain about using filters, on the computer.

Cassy goes back to check the rice. Outside, Dad's car bumps across the field and he parks up next to the caravan. The doors slam.

Kat tumbles in through the caravan door with arm-loads of stuff, followed by a fit-looking dark-haired bloke in neat glasses, and then Dad.

'Better clear the table, Em.' Cassy gets up to greet everyone.

Dan's very polite: he even shakes hands with me, and makes Kat giggle. She's all bubbly and manic.

I put my things away in the bunk room, and lay the table for supper. It's a squash with five people, but Dan doesn't seem bothered. I like him. I can tell he really likes Kat, and that's what matters most to me, more than him being clever or good-looking. But he's both of those too.

'How was London?' Cassy asks as she ladles bean casserole on to five plates. 'Help yourselves to rice.'

'Awesome,' Kat says. She grins at Dan. 'The best time ever.'

'Well, soon be back to the grindstone,' Dad says. 'Won't you have exams this term?'

Kat rolls her eyes. 'End of semester exams, that's all. Not for ages. They don't even count towards your degree.'

'Still, you want to do your best,' Dad says. 'No point doing anything else. What are you studying, Dan?'

'Marine Biology.'

'How fascinating,' Cassy says. 'Do you get to dive and go to coral reefs and swim in lovely exotic warm seas?'

'Later, I can choose to study abroad,' Dan says. 'Canada or New Zealand. It costs extra, though.'

'Worth it,' Dad says. 'You'll already be in debt up to your armpits, I expect!'

'Dad!' Kat frowns at him.

'Tuition fees. Student loans,' Dad says. 'That's all I mean.'

In my head, I'm trying to work out where everyone's going to sleep tonight. Dad and Cassy in the main room, me and Kat on the bunk beds . . . there's not even floor space for Dan. When Kat takes the plates into the kitchenette I follow her.

'Where's Dan going to stay?' I hiss at her.

Kat sighs. 'Duh! We're going on to a party at Mara's, after supper. We'll both stay over there.'

'How was I supposed to know? You never said.'

And that's the end of my chance to tell her about Seb and me. She hardly notices me, she's so set on talking to Dan the whole time. She wants to show him Moat House, but Dad says not in the dark, in the wet.

'You'd better clear up the stuff you've left all over our room,' I say to Kat. 'It's a mess.'

She half-heartedly pushes the bags and rolled-up sleeping bag and stuff on to her bottom bunk, and most of it spills out on to the floor again. And then it's already time for them to go, and with Dan standing right there I can hardly get cross with her about some petty thing like a messy bedroom, so I keep my mouth shut.

'It was good to meet you all,' Dan says. 'Thanks for a lovely supper.'

'You'll be back tomorrow?' Cassy asks Kat.

'Briefly. Then we're getting a lift back to uni from

someone who lives near Bath.'

They've disappeared again all in a whirlwind. Dad drives them to Mara's. Cassy and I are left behind, surveying the general chaos.

'I'll wash, you dry,' Cassy says.

'She doesn't care about anyone except herself, these days,' I grumble.

Cassy laughs. 'Don't take it personally. She's a girl in luuuurve.'

Once we've finished all the piles of washing-up, Cassy lies down on the sofa. She puts both hands on her tummy.

'I'm going to bed,' I say. 'If I can get through the heaps of rubbish she's left.'

'OK, love. School in the morning. Set your alarm, yes?'

I hear Dad come back, not long after, and his low voice talking to Cassy. I hear words like 'essays' and 'she's supposed to be there to study', and Cassy laughing. 'You're such an old crosspatch. Stop stressing about everything. She's just fine.'

Now I'm missing my stupid sister on top of everything else. Even though she is so selfish and horrible sometimes.

Still no texts.

Nothing from Seb.

Nothing from Rachel, even, who's supposed to be revising for her Physics exam.

I lift the curtain to peer out. The rain's stopped at last.

The sofa makes horrible creaking sounds as Dad

and Cassy pull it out to make their bed. Cassy giggles softly. Dad grunts and fusses around.

The fox is back, somewhere beyond the field, calling into the night. I put my hands over my ears.

5

I'm still in a mood when I get back from school the next afternoon. Everyone's out. Kat has left me a note.

Hey dearest Em,
   Sorry we didn't get a chance to talk properly. Why don't you come up to York? Bring beautiful Seb! Have a good term. Good luck with everything. Love you.

And then she's drawn a little cat and two kisses.

PS Sorry about the mess.

I push open the bedroom door. Most of her clothes and stuff have gone, but the duvet's in a tangled heap, and a load of papers and books and things have been shoved half under the bottom bunk. I'm so furious with her I could cry.

But what's the point? So I start sorting it all out. I smooth out the duvet and sheet and put the pillows back in the right place. I stack the books more neatly on the floor, and then I sift the paper into 'rubbish' or 'might be important' piles. It's mostly rubbish, and pages of notes written in blue biro on narrow-lined

159

paper. I put the notes into a plastic sleeve in case she needs them for revision or whatever. I sort through some make-up in case there's anything nice (one lip-gloss, an eyeliner pencil). Then I find a plastic bag with important stuff like her passport and an EU health card, and in with them is her birth certificate. I open it right out. I don't recall ever seeing one before. Dad keeps that sort of thing for all of us in a special file.

The first thing I see, leaping out at me, are the two parents' names handwritten in black ink, one beneath the other.

Father: Robert Michael Woodman
Mother: Francesca Davidson

I stare at the words.

My brain can't make sense of what my eyes are seeing.

Davidson?

I flip out completely.

I don't know how long I sit there. An hour? Two? I get cramp from sitting squashed on the floor for too long. I'm cold to the bone.

All my life – sixteen years of it – I've thought of my mother as Francesca Woodman. Woodman – like Dad and Kat and me: the name that joins us all together, whatever happens.

Davidson?

Why didn't Kat tell me this before? Or Dad? Or *someone*?

Why didn't I think about her using her old name, from before she got married?

I feel totally stupid. Humiliated.

It begins to seep through, the realisation of what this means. How easily I can track her down, now, if I want. Simple as typing a name into a search engine.

I could do it right now.

No wonder nothing came up when I tried before. I was typing in the wrong name.

My heart's thudding.

What am I so scared of?

I fetch my laptop from the table and put it on Kat's bed and switch it on. I take a deep breath. I start to type *Francesca Davidson.*

Francesca Davidson. b. 1971 Canada
Paintings, photography and sculpture:
Natural landscape and domestic portraits form the main subjects of Davidson's work. A bold sequence of paintings of women in domestic settings were exhibited in the Musée d'art moderne 2007 . . .

I find five references to her work in total. All her exhibited work is in France. So that's where she must be living, mustn't it?

I'm shaking all over. My head's a jumbled mess. I switch off the laptop, shove the birth certificate back with the other stuff in the bag, grab my coat and phone.

I try Seb's mobile one more time. Nothing. So I dial his home number.

Avril answers. I can tell she's surprised to hear my voice.

'Is Seb there?' I ask.

'No , Em. He's not coming back here at all while he's on the course. It's good that it's going so well, isn't it? We're so pleased.'

Course? When did he decide on that?

I don't know what to say.

'So,' Avril says. 'How can I help, Emily?'

I think fast. I can't bear her to know that Seb has told me nothing about what he's doing. 'His mobile doesn't seem to be working. So I thought I'd check with you . . .' I know how feeble I sound even as the words come out.

'That's odd. He phoned us yesterday without any problem. He's probably run out of credit or something. I can give you Ruby's number, if you hang on,' Avril says. 'Try him there, Emily. He's probably busy during the day, but later this evening he'll be at Ruby's, I should think. Unless they all go down the pub at the end of the day!'

I write down the number. 'Thanks,' I say. 'Bye, Avril.' My hands are shaking.

So.

Seb's doing his stone-carving course. The one he talked about.

Seb's away, for six weeks? Or longer? And he didn't tell me?

I'm trembling all over.

I can't bear it.

I sit there for ages, frozen.

I phone Rachel. 'Can I come over?' I say. 'I need to talk to you. Please? I won't stay long. I know you've got your exam tomorrow.'

I start the long walk up to the bus stop.

Rachel's sitting on her bed, surrounded by bits of paper and small notecards with tiny writing on in different colours. I pick one up.

'You can test me on those,' Rachel says.

'OK. What's the formula for Work?'

'Work equals Force times Distance.'

I pick up the next card. 'Power equals?'

'Power equals Work (energy transferred) over Time.'

It makes no sense to me whatsoever.

'So. What's happened? Seb?' Rachel asks.

'Seb, and something else.'

'You're pregnant!'

'NO! How could I possibly be . . . Honestly, Rachel!'

'What, then? Your eyes are all bloodshot. You look terrible.'

'I've found out something about my real mother . . .'

'Your mother Francesca?'

'Yes.'

'About time!' Rachel says. 'How come?'

I tell her about the birth certificate, and about what I found on the internet. 'She's an artist. I think she lives in France. Her real name is Francesca Davidson.'

163

'That's it?'

'So far.'

'Great. Well, it's a start.'

'I feel all shaky and funny. Like, it's made her real. She's a real person, and out there!'

'Of course.'

Rachel's phone bleeps. She checks the message. 'Luke,' she says. 'Hang on a minute; I'll just answer him quickly.'

I wait.

She turns back to me. 'Why's her name different, do you reckon? Perhaps your dad and her weren't actually married.'

'Or she kept her own name. Like, lots of artists and writers and people do that, don't they? Why should you change your name, anyway? Just because you're the woman?'

Rachel shrugs. 'What's the big deal about a name? So, are you going to contact her or what?'

'Do you think I should?'

Rachel makes a big effort. Half of her brain is still thinking *Luke,* or possibly (unlikely) *Physics.* 'Of course! I've thought that for ages. You're bound to feel a bit strange, right now. So let it sink in. There's no hurry, is there? You've waited all these years. A few days won't make any difference. Wait till after the exams.'

She's so sensible and rational I begin to calm down too. She's right. What's the rush?

'And Seb's gone away,' I say. 'We had a terrible row.' I tell her what happened. All the sordid details.

164

'Why didn't you tell me about this before?' Rachel asks. 'You are such an idiot, sometimes, Em. I knew something was the matter with you. I assumed it was the exams, or the caravan or something.'

Amanda comes upstairs with two cups of tea. 'Revision?' she says, looking at Rachel. 'Don't blow it now. Sorry, Emily, but Rachel needs to do some work.'

I get up. 'I was just going, in any case,' I say. 'I've got work to do too. And my bus goes in five minutes.'

Cassy and Dad are in the middle of supper by the time I get back to the caravan.

'All right?' Cassy says. 'I assumed you'd eaten? Wherever you've been.'

'Rachel's,' I say. 'And I'm not hungry.'

'It's not too much to ask, is it, that you leave us a note at least, to say where you are?' Dad says through a mouthful of spaghetti.

'Sorry,' I say. 'Sorry sorry sorry. That enough?'

I slam the bedroom door. It clicks to, annoyingly softly.

I try talking to Kat on MSN.

– I found your birth certificate. Our mother's name is on it. Why didn't you tell me??????

– *You've been going through my stuff?* she types back.

– YOU left it in a mess. In MY room.

– *What's the matter?*

– The name. Francesca DAVIDSON??? I never knew.

– *And the big deal is?*

– How can you say that? It's a HUGE deal. It changes everything.

– *I don't see why. It's just a surname, for God's sake.*

– It means I can find out who she is.

– *DON'T.*

– Why not? Aren't you curious too?

– *NO. She's nothing to do with us.*

– I want to find her.

My words hang there. I wait ages for Kat to answer. Finally she starts typing again.

– *I'm getting on fine with my life without her. I don't need her messing it up again. Nor do you.*

Then she's off-line. I can't even answer back.

I read back the typed conversation. My own words surprise me. *I want to find her.* I typed that sentence without a thought, and the real truth came out. I want to find her. I want to see her, what she's like. I want to know everything about her.

I search through Kat's box of books on the shelf, and fish out the faded book of fairy tales. I open the front cover, trace my finger around the name, like Kat and I used to do. *Francesca.*

Who on earth is she?

What kind of mother leaves two small children, and doesn't even try to tell them why?

I try one more time, searching back through all my memories, to find one of her. Just the tiniest fragment. The feel of her arm, or the smell of her perfume, or the sound of her voice.

Nothing.

All I have are the memories of *afterwards,* of Kat and me in the garden, eating raspberries and redcurrants, Kat reading to me and telling me stories.

I try to imagine it. I close my eyes and concentrate hard.

That last day, before she went. Because there would have been a day like that, a day before leaving, when she did ordinary things with me and Kat, like any ordinary mum. Making breakfast. Washing-up. Getting us dressed. Walking to the shops, me in a buggy and Kat holding the handle. Did she take us to the park? Push us on the swings? Or was it a truly terrible day, both of us yelling and squabbling, endless rain, no car, Dad at work till late, like he always was, night after night? Francesca bored bored bored, frustrated and lonely, the artist who can't paint, can't take photos, desperate and at the end of her tether.

How bad would it have to be, to make you leave everything?

I lie awake for ages, thinking about what I've found out today.

It's like someone's lifted off the top of my head and let in all this air. I'm dizzy with it.

6

'Want to come to Moat House at the weekend? See the latest developments?' Dad says over supper on Thursday. 'They've worked fast these last couple of weeks.'

Cassy looks at him. 'How about if we go and get Mattie first, and bring her with us? Instead of a walk, she can just have a run around.'

'Good idea,' Dad says. 'What do you think, Em?'

'It depends,' I say. 'Are we going to adopt her or not? And if not, what's the point? It'll just make me sad.'

'You know we can't have her yet,' Cassy says. 'It doesn't make any sense. But when we move into Moat House, things will be different. Rob and I've talked about it. There is lots of room, what with the garden, and the field. You were right about that. It's a good place for a dog.'

'Is that a yes, then?'

'It's a *probably*,' Cassy says. 'That's as much as I can promise at the moment.'

My eyes sting with sudden tears. Perhaps things will work out for Mattie, at least.

*   *   *

Mattie sits on the seat in the back of the car with me, her head resting in my lap. She's trembling, as if she's afraid. Or cold. I stroke her silky ears, and run my hand over her spine. You can feel all the bones, and even though I know she's that kind of dog, I can't help thinking she's way too skinny. But she perks up when we get out of the car, and she dashes across the garden like a coiled spring, newly released, charging through the big puddles and running round in ever-increasing circles. We walk up the steps to the front door, and when I call her, Mattie comes racing back.

'She remembers you all right,' Cassy says. 'It's good to see that.'

The beautiful oak front door has been restored and has a proper lock on it. Inside, the house smells of new wood instead of damp and decay. The floorboards have been laid upstairs; electric cables are being installed. In the centre of the big front room, the new staircase winds round in a spiral to the first floor. The French windows are in place, so the house is flooded with light. Cassy and Dad go into the kitchen together. Cassy's making little exclaiming sounds. 'Oh . . . oh, Rob . . . It's just lovely!' I watch Dad; he stands behind Cassy, puts his arms around her, his hands over her belly. He nuzzles his face into her hair. They don't need me. They've forgotten I'm here, even.

Mattie whines to go back outside and I go with her. I close the door softly behind me and follow her down to the river. It's still high, up almost to the top of the banks, and beyond it, the field gleams silver, another lake. The geese I saw with Seb have all gone. Mattie

169

sniffs along the bank, tail low and quivering, following some scent trail. She scuffs through the dead leaves beneath the willows, and then slips under the fence into the copse of trees.

I can't get it out of my head: that image of Dad and Cassy and the new baby. The new family who will live in this perfect house, when it's finished, all clean and made new. The house is coming awake again, everything starting over, afresh. But it all looks so different to me, now. I can't feel excited about any of it.

When Seb and I came here that first time and we climbed the scaffolding to my attic room, and we pushed the skylight wide open to let in the night, and when we first kissed . . . it was as if everything was thrilling. Everything was about to happen. I was excited about the house, about Seb, about me . . .

And now it's not like that. It's like everything's been spoiled.

I turn when I hear footsteps.

'There you are!' Dad comes over, a clipboard in his hand. 'Want to see the early plans for out here?'

He's oblivious to what I'm feeling. He just ploughs on, regardless. 'Wondered about having a dovecote, a traditional circular stone tower, just here.' He points to the place on the plan with his pencil. 'Like the one at Minster Lovell. Remember? You loved it, when you were little.'

I do remember. The sound of the doves echoed round the tower when I ducked through the little door and crouched inside. Small white feathers drifted down from the rafters, and it was warm in the summer sun. And Kat was calling for me, looking for me all over the gardens, while I stayed curled up, hidden and happy in my secret place . . .

Dad's still talking. '. . . formal kitchen gardens, up near the house, with box hedges, but we'll let it all run a bit wild down to the river . . . daffodils and fritillaries in the long grass. Cowslips and foxgloves . . .'

I don't say a word.

Dad finally stops. 'What's the matter with you?' he asks. His voice is strained, edged with irritation.

I shrug. He hates that.

'Emily!'

'What?'

'Can't you show a bit more interest? A bit of enthusiasm? Aren't you excited about all this? The house? You were, before.'

Before.

Exactly.

Before the baby. Before I started finding things out about Francesca. Before I argued with Seb. Before Kat got close to Dan and couldn't be bothered with me any more.

'It doesn't feel like my house any more,' I mumble.

'It's a mess, I know, with the builders' stuff all over the place, but it's getting better all the time. You wait and see. It's going to be fabulous.'

'It's not that,' I say.

'What, then?'

'It's you. Cassy and you and the baby. That's who the house belongs to really. That's what it's been

171

about all along. Only I didn't see that before.'

'How can you say that? You mustn't think that!'

'But I do.'

'Hey, Em. Come here.' He tries to put his arm round me.

I pull away. I stare at the brown water, the branches being swirled downstream in the fast flow of the river.

'Emily?' Dad isn't going to let it go. 'Listen to me. The baby doesn't change the way I feel about you and Kat.'

'NO? You listen to ME, for once!' I shout, suddenly furious. All that pent-up emotion I've been holding on to, deep inside, comes boiling up. 'You never tell me the truth about anything. You never have. You've never once thought about what it's like for me. Living with you and Cassy. Always having to move house because of YOUR stupid plans and your stupid houses. Living in a caravan, for God's sake, in the middle of winter, miles from everyone, in the middle of a muddy field.'

Dad's staring at me, but I can't stop. I'm on a roll.

'And that's not the worst thing. Not by a million miles. All these years and years and you've never had the guts to tell me the truth about my mother. Never talked about her or told me why she went or where she is now. You never even told me her real name.'

Dad steps back. It makes me want to hit him.

'You could have told me that, don't you think? One little thing about her NAME. Francesca DAVIDSON! Hah!' I spit the words out, hurl them like stones. 'Can

172

you imagine what it's like, to suddenly find that out, when you are sixteen? No. Because you're too much of a coward. Because you never think about anyone except yourself.'

'That's not true –' Dad starts to defend himself, but his phone rings at the same moment.

I can't believe what he does next. He actually pulls his phone out of his pocket and checks to see who it is! And then he answers it. The final insult.

'Cassy? What's up?' He turns away from me to talk to her.

That's how it's always going to be. Clear as anything, I see how it will be from now on. Cassy first. Cassy-and-baby first.

I start running.

Dad calls after me. 'Emily? Wait a moment. We will talk about it . . . just let me sort this out and then –'

'Piss off, Dad.'

I skid in the mud, fumble my way under the willow trees, climb through the barbed-wire fence into the copse where Mattie went after the rabbits. My jacket gets snagged on the wire and I have to unhook it, before I can start running again, pushing through the wet branches and brambles and undergrowth, my face wet and my eyes smarting.

A huge bird rears up from a dead branch and flaps away noisily over the treetops. I keep running and crying and stumbling, my jeans sopping and my boots muddy and disgusting, until I'm out of breath and shaking, my heart thumping so loud it makes my ears ring.

I finally stop, and listen. Silence closes in. No traffic sounds, or birds even. Just a faint dripping sound of rain on leaves. No sound of Dad crashing after me through the undergrowth. No chance, then, of carrying on shouting and hurting him and getting it all out of me, letting go of all those horrible thoughts and feelings, saying all the cooped-up words at last.

Instead, he's obviously gone back to talk to Cassy about the house. Even the house is more important than me.

I lean back against the wet bark of an oak tree. My feet slip in the dead leaves at the base of the trunk and I let myself slide, down to earth, till I'm actually sitting on the wet ground, my back against the tree. I hug my knees.

I'm just another wet thing in the wet wood, almost the same colour, now, with all the mud and the rain and the bits of twig and dead stuff caught on my jacket and in my hair.

The rain turns to a fine drizzle. It drips through the tree on to my head and shoulders. I don't move. The rain finally stops, although every time the wind moves the branches a fine spray spatters down. Still I crouch there.

Nearby, a bird starts to sing. I can actually see its throat quivering as it opens its beak. Other birds join in. It's like the wood comes alive again. Some creature rustles through the dead leaves under the bramble thicket. A woodpecker hammers the trunk of a tree some way off. Now the rain has stopped I can hear the rush of the river as it tumbles over the weir further down the valley.

Another time. A different wood. Kat and me, playing under an oak tree while Dad is – where? I can't remember. Just the waiting for him to come back, and a sort of worry in my belly: he's been too long. Kat peels the bark off a stick. I watch a line of ants march single file across the corner of the blanket, holding their tiny burden of crumbs above their heads. A column of flies rise and fall in flight together. A background hum of insect life. The smell of peaty earth: leaf mould. I take a stick and drill it down into the sweet rich earth, down through the layers of rotting leaves, one autumn over another, down to the soil dark as coffee grounds.

That's what memory is like: layers, one overlapping another, and compacting down the way old leaves slowly crumble and turn to a rich peaty soil, nourishing the new things that will grow. It's why it's important, remembering things. It's why it matters, when the memories aren't there, and no one fill in the gaps for you.

A twig snaps. I'm suddenly alert, watchful. A swishing sound: feet moving through wet grass. I stay as still as I can, hunched against my tree, arms round my knees, blending into the life of the woods.

A fox? A person?

I let my breath out slowly.

I see Dad before he sees me. He looks tired, and old, his face somehow not yet ready, not expecting to be seen.

'Dad?'

He stops; he looks baffled for the second before he sees me, camouflaged against the tree. He comes over. 'Found a dry spot?' he says.

'Not really. It's OK.'

He hunkers down beside me. We don't speak.

I'm not angry, now I see Dad. I'm just glad he's here. That he did come to find me, after all.

'Did we live near some woods a bit like these, once?' I say. 'Did Kat and I play there?'

'A long, long time ago. Fancy you remembering that. You were very little,' Dad says.

'I'm not sure what I remember,' I say, 'and what I've been told. Kat used to tell me things.'

Dad thinks for a while. 'Sometimes we went for walks at the weekends. We pushed you in the buggy as far as the bridge, then I carried you on my shoulders, up into the woods. You and Kat played on the rug, and I picked blackberries, or just walked a bit further.' He looks at me. 'It was after your mother left.'

His words hang there between us. All the pain and sadness in that little word: *left*.

Is he going to talk about her at last? I sit very still, not wanting to disturb this moment, waiting and hoping.

Dad clears his throat. He starts talking again. 'Everything was a struggle. I was beside myself. Two small daughters and a full-time job and not a clue why she'd gone, how she could do such a thing. The selfishness of it was breathtaking.' He picks at a twig.

He doesn't notice the thorns, the beads of blood oozing along a fine tear in the skin on his hand.

'I know we messed up, Francesca and I. But I did the best I could, then and ever since, Em. And you and Kat have come through it all just fine. Better than fine. Francesca said you'd be better off without her, and perhaps she was right, after all. You and Kat stopped talking about her pretty soon, at least. Stopped asking for her.'

For a moment I glimpse us: little Emily and not-much-bigger Katharine. Waking in the night, calling for our mummy in the darkness. And she doesn't come, however much we call. Dad, tears wet on his cheeks, holding us, one arm around each, and the night light making a yellow moon on the bedroom wall.

Is it a real memory? Or a picture I make for myself, out of the dark?

Dad keeps talking. 'Your mother fell for someone. She said he made her complete, in a way I never had, never could. That with him she could be the woman she really was. The woman and the artist. He was an artist too, of course. But he didn't have children. Children didn't fit in with his scheme of things.'

Dad looks at me. 'I've kept my mouth shut about your mother all these years because I promised myself I wouldn't dump all my bitterness and anger about her on to you and Kat. Because she is still your mother, in name at least.'

'Not even in name,' I say. 'We don't even share the same name.'

Dad sighs. 'Davidson was simply her name before we married, and she didn't see why she should change it. Lots of women feel like that. I didn't mind. It didn't seem important.'

'But you should have told me,' I say. 'You should have said something.'

Dad sits up a bit straighter. 'It's cold here. Are you ready to go back?'

I can't bear to stop now. All the things I want to know . . .

'What did she look like?' I say. 'Tell me about her.'

He thinks for a bit. 'A little like Kat, a lot like you. Dark, and pretty.'

I don't think of me as being pretty. I don't want to be. It makes people like you for the wrong reasons. I want people to like me because I'm me, not because of what I look like. In any case, everyone says Kat is the *pretty* one.

Dad stands up and brushes the leaves off his coat. 'Come on, Em. Time to head back. Cassy's already overdone it today. We need to take care of her a bit more, with the baby and everything.' His voice changes, not sad, now, but confident, assertive. The usual Dad. 'She means the world to me, Em. You have got to understand that. When Cassy came along, she turned things back to good. I was scared I might lose everything. Lose you and Kat. She made life seem possible again. She did a great job helping bring you two up. And I don't want to start upsetting her now, raking up the past, talking about Francesca.'

So. That's it, then? Dad's closing down. Our little

window of intimacy has shut again.

'You go. I'll come back later,' I say.

'You'll have to make your own way back, then,' Dad says.

I watch him going back under the trees. His footsteps get fainter. He doesn't look back once.

7

Emily Woodman c/o Moat House

I pick up the envelope from the caravan table and stare at the unfamiliar handwriting on the front. Who would write to me at Moat House? And instantly I know, and my heart's hammering against my ribs and I snatch the envelope up and go to lie on the top bunk to open it, where no one can see.

Inside is a postcard with an aerial view of the Island of Portland, and a cross marked in blue biro on a cliff on one side. I turn it over.

It's good here – hard work though . . . The course is brilliant and I've met some amazing people . . . I've learned how to do lettering and different techniques for cutting and carving stone by hand. There is a prison on the island and it's all a bit grey and cold but interesting. The actual quarry is extraordinary . . . It makes me think about your idea of photography as a kind of drawing with light. When the sun shines, the stone is like a block of light and cutting it with the chisel, you make lines of darkness and shadow. (Poetic enough for you?) I am sorry we fell out. Still don't really get it. Sorry

180

I went off without telling you. Hope you are OK. Missing you.
Love Seb

I read it over and over. I pick out the words I want to hear. *Sorry. Missing you. Love.*

I tuck the card between the pages of the blue and gold notebook, to keep it safe.

I find my school pencil case, take out my ink pen, rummage through my stack of photographs to find one to send back like a postcard. I choose one of the little Christmas tree. I phone Avril to get Auntie Ruby's address.

Thanks for your card. Really glad you like your course. Missing you too. Sorry about how I was. Lots more to tell you. See you soon.
Em xxx

I take a deep breath. Perhaps there's a way Seb and I can work things out, after all. I let myself begin to hope.

8

To: emilywoodman2
From: katkin

Hello Em! How are you? I've got a bad cold and too much work! Missed all my lectures this week. Don't tell Dad. Got to bed at 3 a.m. last night cos we went to an awesome new club. Have u and Seb made up? Forget about looking for F. I mean it. We don't need her messing everything up now.

Lots of love K xx

I'm about to email Kat back when Cassy stumbles through the door and dumps a cardboard box on the table in the caravan.

'Should you be carrying that?' I say.

'Probably not! Don't tell Rob. It's something I wanted to do for you. I went to the storage place. Found it eventually.'

'What is it?'

'Come and take a look.' Cassy's grinning wildly.

I untie the string and lift the flaps of the box.

Inside, I find two albums and a stack of loose photographs. 'For my project?' I ask Cassy, confused.

She shakes her head. 'It might fill some of the gaps. I don't really know what's in there, but they're from when you were a baby. They might help . . . with memories and stuff. From when you were little. Your dad told me you were asking.'

She leaves me there while she puts the kettle on and starts making tea. She curls up on the sofa with her pregnancy book, and leaves me to get on with it by myself.

The photos are a mix: Kat and me, Cassy and Dad. School photos, boring studio-type photos of us in school uniform. Holiday snaps; sandy beaches, Kat and me playing, a very young-looking Cassy doing cartwheels along the sand, and Kat and me trying to copy her, all of us grinning at the camera. I don't remember that holiday though. It's like looking at someone else's life. There are lots of photos of houses: places we've lived over the years, places we've stayed for holidays. One I stare at for ages, because the garden looks so familiar: the square lawn, and the tree in the middle, and the vegetable garden behind, with rows of currant bushes. It's the garden from the memory, Kat reading to me.

The albums I don't remember seeing before. There have always been a few framed photos of us as babies, stuck up round the houses we've lived in, but these are proper albums like hard-backed books. I pick up the blue one, study the handwriting along the label on the spine: the fine looping letters. It's a grown-up version of the writing in our story book: Francesca's hand, shaping the letters for *Katharine Jane. 7 July*.

I glance at Cassy. She's immersed in her book. I turn over the first page of the album. Two photographs fill the page. The first is black and white. It shows a newborn baby lying in a basket, a shaft of sunlight catching her hand. The light picks out fine details: the texture of the quilt, the weave of the basket, the soft baby skin. In the second picture, in colour this time, the same baby – Kat – is being held over someone's shoulder, so Kat's little round face is peeping at the camera, her eyes blue and wide open. The shoulder belongs to a woman in a turquoise short-sleeved dress. You can see the back of her head: long, dark hair in a loose plait.

I start to feel dizzy.

I make myself turn over the page.

There she is again. Wavy dark hair, loose in this photo, falling forward as she bends her head down, feeding the baby. She's looking down at the baby – at Kat – rather than at the camera. On the opposite page she's looking straight at whoever is taking the picture, smiling, as if they are in mid-conversation.

I stare at her for a long time.

She smiles back, her mouth half open in speech.

It's the strangest thing. I'm looking at Francesca, and I don't feel a rush of recognition, or any feeling other than intense curiosity. As if she's a puzzle I'm trying to unravel, a secret code I need to decipher.

It gets easier, turning the pages. There aren't that many of Francesca, and gradually I work out that it must be her who's taking the photographs. They're very good: not your average snapshots like most of the loose photos in the box from later on, but taken with a proper quality camera, single lens reflex, by someone who understands about light, and composition, and then has developed them herself.

My mother the photographer.

I pick up the second album. On the cream spine the label says, *Emily Anna. 21 June.*

There are fewer photos in this album. There's one of me in the same basket, the same pale blue quilt with white rabbits, as Kat. Me propped up against cushions, in a chair. One family one, taken perhaps on a timer, because Kat, Dad and Francesca have the sort of rigid smile you might have if you've had to wait a while for the shutter. Dad's holding me. I'm wrapped in a lacy shawl. Kat, a toddler, sits on Francesca's lap, one hand against the side of Francesca's mouth as if she's trying to stop her speaking.

I study all the pictures of Francesca, trying to find some clue about what she's feeling, but I can't tell.

'All right?' Cassy says from the sofa. 'Found anything?'

'Some of me as a baby. And lots of Kat.'

'And Francesca?'

'Yes.'

'Want to show me?'

'If you like.'

I wonder guiltily what Dad would say. But Cassy

seems completely fine about it. Maybe Dad's wrong about her. Maybe, after all, it's just Dad who gets upset about Francesca, not Cassy.

'She's very attractive,' Cassy says. We peer into Francesca's face, both of us. 'No wonder that bloke fell in love with her.'

'What was his name? Do you know?'

'He was French, I think. Pierre? Something like that. It made your dad so angry that even all these years later he can hardly speak about it. As you may have noticed. It almost destroyed him.'

'Where are they now?'

'I've no idea. She never wrote or phoned or anything, as far as I know. I couldn't understand it. How she could just vanish out of her children's lives. Such a selfish thing to do!'

'She must have had her reasons,' I say, starting to pile the photos and albums back into the box. Suddenly I don't want to hear Cassy's opinions of my mother.

I put all the photos back except one. I slip it into my pocket for now; later I'll put it in the notebook. It's one I didn't show Cassy, of an older Francesca in a blue sleeveless dress, in front of a house. A big stone house with a woodpile along one wall, and a balcony under an upstairs window. She's holding a grey tabby cat in her arms, and she's looking directly at the camera, her face relaxed and open. The light is strong sunlight, but with long shadows, as if it's late afternoon, somewhere hot.

It's another piece of the puzzle.

She must have sent that afterwards, later. And for some reason, Dad kept it safe.

Cassy and I hide the box in my room with all the other stuff under Kat's bunk.

'I'll smuggle it back to the store sometime when your dad's not around,' Cassy says. 'He doesn't need to know.'

'Why would he mind? They're only photos,' I say.

Cassy sighs heavily. 'They are memories, aren't they? They stir things up. It's complicated. He was badly hurt. You know that, Em.'

'But it's my past too, and I need to know.'

'Yes. I understand that. I'll try and talk to him about it. But not at the moment. Not while he's so stressed and busy.'

They are as bad as each other, I think. Each thinking they're protecting the other. Neither of them can really think about *me*, what *I* need.

'It's weird to think of all our stuff in the store,' I say. 'I've got used to not having anything.'

Cassy laughs. 'Really? I can't wait to get it all back out and moved into Moat House. I hate living like this.'

'How long will it be, do you think?'

'Another four months, perhaps? Before the baby, I hope.'

'There's loads to do, still.'

'Even when the builders and stonemasons and carpenters are finished, there's all the plastering and decorating and kitchen fittings and the bathrooms.'

Cassy looks exhausted at the thought of it all. 'Plus the garden to sort from scratch. It's a total mess. Can you imagine, bringing up a baby in a virtual building site?'

'It'll be all right,' I say. 'The baby won't mind.'

'Won't it?' Cassy starts laughing again, and then for some reason she's got tears in her eyes and is crying too, all mixed up.

I put my arms round her. She seems too young to be having a baby, even at thirty-one. There's something about her that won't ever grow up. Perhaps that's one of the things Dad loves about her. Cassy won't ever leave. She'll always need him.

'Just look at me! What a state!' Cassy blows her nose and brushes herself down. Little bits of fluff from the carpet are stuck all over her trousers.

'You'll need new clothes soon,' I say. 'Bigger ones.'

'You could come with me to choose,' Cassy says. 'We could get some baby things too. Would you, Em? I'd love that. Please?'

'OK,' I say. 'If you like.'

I think about the baby in the basket. Baby Kat and then Baby Em. Perhaps stacked in the pile of all our things in the store is the same old Moses basket, and Cassy's baby will sleep in it too.

'When will you know if it's a boy or a girl?'

'I don't want to know,' Cassy says. 'I want to wait till we meet face to face, when it's born.' She looks at me, her eyes still glittery with tears. 'It's started to move around,' she says. 'So I know it really is there, after all. To begin with, I couldn't quite believe it was real. That it would stay.'

Cassy gets up stiffly from the floor. 'Rob'll be back any minute. Better warm him up some dinner.'

I stay in my room, so I can think about everything.

And just before I go to sleep, a text comes at last, from Seb.

Got your card. C U soon. 2 more weeks. xxxx

9

'19th February. Twenty weeks.' Cassy is reading aloud from her pregnancy book. 'You will notice your baby being more active and may even be able to see some of its movements. The baby is now about twenty-five centimetres long.'

I stop getting ready for a moment and find my pencil case and a ruler, so we can see exactly how big that is. Cassy's bump is really obvious now, especially when she pulls her stripy T-shirt down tight over her tummy.

'Where're you off to?' Cassy asks me.

'Meeting Seb.'

'When did he get back?'

'Today.'

'Expect you've missed him. Six weeks is a long time.'

I don't answer. I check my hair and grab my bag from the table.

'You look lovely,' Cassy says. 'Have a nice time. But don't be too late tonight, Em. You've got school tomorrow.'

*   *   *

He's waiting for me at the gate. We said we'd meet at seven at the top of the lane, so he must've been early. Seeing him there, the real flesh and blood Seb with his dark hair and black jacket and stripy scarf wound loosely round, my brain does a kind of double-take. I've thought about him so much that seeing him for real is almost a shock, as if my imagined Seb and the real one have to merge together. He's so warm and solid and alive and beautiful!

'Hey, you!' he says. He wraps me in his arms, and we hug tight. I bury my face into his chest, breathe in fully the smell of him.

'Missed you!' he says into my hair, muffling the words.

We hold each other at arm's length so we can see each other properly.

'Missed you too,' I say.

We kiss. It's like that first time. Like going underwater and coming up for air, my skin tingly, little shivers running up and down my backbone. His mouth is hot and damp and hungry.

'Was it good? Did you learn lots? Did you pass?' I ask as we walk hand-in-hand up the lane to the car.

'It was amazing,' Seb says. 'Yes, I passed the Level One test. I can go back there at Easter and do the next level, and eventually I can get a qualification from the college, as good as a degree. Better, really, because I can get a proper job with it.'

'Bet your mum's happy,' I say.

'Yeah. She's over the moon. Dad too, except he doesn't say much. I can tell, though.' Seb grins. 'Mum blames you. She thinks it's because of you that I got things together. She says you gave me *focus*.'

That makes me go all tingly and warm inside.

'I made you something,' Seb says. ' A sort of sorry present. I thought a lot about you being so upset. And how I was. I don't want it to be like that again.'

I swallow hard. 'Me neither. I'm sorry too.'

We've reached the car. Seb unlocks the doors and we climb in. He leans over to get something from the shelf under the dashboard. 'For you,' he says, and puts a small paper parcel on my lap.

It's heavy for such a small thing. I unwrap the layers of newspaper.

'It's Portland stone,' Seb says.

I cradle it in my palm: a small mouse made of limestone, smooth as an egg, with ears and paws and lines for whiskers and a curled-up stone tail and everything. It's the perfect shape to sit in my hand. After a while, the stone seems to warm up, as if the mouse is coming alive.

'Thank you!' The words don't seem big enough, to say what I really feel. 'It's perfect.'

'It took ages. But it isn't perfect. It's hard to work on such a small scale. And you have to go with the stone. There are fossils and stuff in it. See?'

I keep the stone mouse in my hands all the way to his house. I shall keep it safe for ever.

'Will your mum and dad be there?' I ask, as we get to the edge of the village.

'Later. But they're down the pub at the moment.'

* * *

192

I'm a bit nervous, still. We lie on Seb's bed and listen to music. We lie close, and we kiss, and we talk a lot. He tells me more about Portland, and Auntie Ruby, and about the course. I tell him about Francesca, what I've found. He listens and doesn't interrupt. We are both on our best behaviour, I think; scared of making another mistake. But we can't carry on like that. So I launch in.

'I know you wanted to help me, before,' I explain, 'with finding Francesca. But I worked out that I have to do it my own way. Like, I have to be in control of it all. The timing, and everything.'

He nods, as if he's trying to understand. 'Well,' he says. 'I still will help, if you want me to. But you'll have to say, if you do. And it's OK if you don't.'

We hear his parents come home. When we go down to the kitchen Avril dances over and puts her arms round us both. 'Hello, lovebirds!'

Seb pushes her away. 'Leave it out, Mum. How much have you had to drink?'

But I don't really mind. I fill the kettle and Seb gets four blue spotty mugs out for tea. It's cosy in the kitchen, and everything looks shiny and bright.

'Good to see you here again, Emily,' Nick says to me in his gruff way, before he goes through to the lounge and switches on the telly. Avril goes upstairs to run a bath.

'Shall I take you back, then?' Seb says.

He stops the car at the gate to the caravan field. He puts his arms round me, and we kiss again, but it feels different, this time. What would it be like, I wonder, to spend all night together? Not now, not yet, but sometime?

'I'm so glad you're back,' I say. 'I missed you so much.'

'I'll have to go away again,' Seb says.

'Yes, I know. You said at Easter. And that's OK too. That's just the way it has to be. But next time we won't argue and not make up, first. I don't want us ever to do that again.'

'OK.'

'And it's not as if I haven't got my own projects to do,' I say. 'So don't think I'll be moping at home all the time you're gone. I'll be getting ready for my exams. Photography practical: eight hours of it. As well as English and Geography.' I get out of the car, lean forward to talk to him through the open window. 'And soon after that, I'll be moving into Moat House. Imagine that!'

Kat and Rachel and I have talked loads of times, about how you'll know when you find true love. The chance in a million of meeting the right person for you, the one you want to be with for ever. Rachel reckons that there must be hundreds of people who could be right, with a bit of effort that is, on both sides: she says it's what you make of a relationship that counts.

Kat thinks some people are a lot more right than others, obviously, and maybe there *is* just one who is the perfect match, the one who is your soulmate, the other half of you that makes you whole.

And if Kat is right, how lucky does that make me? Because with absolute certainty I know I have found him.

Seb.

Our one-in-a-million chance, and we've found each other.

Lying in bed, my hand on the stone mouse next to me on the sheet, that's what I'm thinking as I slip towards sleep.

It's a cold, clear night with a moon. The vixen is calling across the field. The sound makes me shiver. It seems so close I must surely be able to see her this time. I lift the curtain edge, peer out into the moonlit night. My breath mists the window glass. I rub it clear again with the corner of the sheet.

Is that her, stepping out of the shadows at the edge of the field? I can't be sure. The eerie cry of the fox weaves its way into my dreams.

10

Late February. Seb and I climb over the stile and then let Mattie off the lead. She runs in excited rings around us and then bounds ahead down the footpath. She knows the way, we've taken her that many times since the weather got better. It's half-term; Rachel's in Paris with Amanda. I'm glad, now, that I haven't gone with them. I'm saving up all my money for another trip, in the summer: a journey just beginning to take its shadowy shape in my mind.

Some of the trees are beginning to get the first flush of green. The wood smells of wild garlic. I want to take a new sequence of photos, today, now it's almost spring. I chuck a stick for Mattie and she chases after it half-heartedly, before finding some more interesting scent to follow. We go after her, off the path down the smaller animal track downhill under the trees to our special place with the fallen log, where the sun shines on to a patch of mossy grass and no one ever comes but us.

Seb takes his coat off and lays it down for us to lie on. 'Got your camera?'

'Of course.'

He dozes while I take my photographs. Already the light is different, the sun higher in the sky. In three weeks it will be the spring equinox, and the clocks will go forward, and it will be light later into the evening.

The sun falling through the canopy of branches and twigs and tight-curled leaf buds makes a criss-cross pattern on the grass. I make Seb move so that the pattern falls on his face. He closes his eyes again. I click and click, a whole black and white film. He lies on his back, one arm curved above his head, the way a baby sleeps: open and trusting. The light shifts, edges away. *Click. Click.* I watch him through the camera lens, see him in microscopic detail. Eyelashes on his cheek. The curve of his neck. The edge of his upper lip, the dark shadow round his jaw.

Mattie curls round tight against his back, and she sleeps too.

It's the hardest thing, taking her back to the dogs' home and leaving her. I hear Mattie whine as she's shut back in her pen.

'I wish we could bring her home right now instead of waiting,' I say to Seb.

Back in the car, I get my photo of Francesca out again, smooth out the creases. 'It looks a bit like a farmhouse, doesn't it? There's a hay meadow at the side, I think. And the huge woodpile. And it looks hot.'

'Why don't you write to the gallery where her work was displayed?' Seb says. 'They must have her address. It's not rocket science, Em, if you really want to find her, this time.'

'I do.'

'You're sure?'

'Yes.'

'Will you tell your dad?'

'Not yet. I want to find her first. By myself.'

I know my way of doing things sometimes makes Seb impatient with me, but that's the way it's going to be. He has to get used to it.

I go round to Rachel's when she's back from Paris, so she can help me with the words on the French website for the Musée d'art moderne in Céret, near the Pyrenees.

'I looked for photos by Francesca in the museum we went to in Paris,' Rachel says. 'But I didn't find anything.'

I scroll down the list of references to Francesca to show Rachel. We click on the museum website.

Rachel reads it out for me. 'OK, then. We'll send them an email, yes? What do you want to say?'

I dictate, and Rachel translates into her best A-level-standard French, which is a million times better than my GCSE grade C. I keep changing my mind what to say. In the end, I say, *I'm a student of Photography. I'm doing a project. I want to see more of Francesca Davidson's work and would like to contact her. Please let me have her address.*

'Everything is true,' I say to Rachel. 'Even if it's not the whole truth.'

'You're sure? Final chance?'

'Yes.'

We click Send.

No reply comes whizzing back, of course. We lie on Rachel's bed, and she talks about Luke, and Paris, and Amanda. Eventually it's time for me to get the bus home.

I'm working on my English homework, three days later, when the *new mail* message flashes up.

It's from the gallery, I can tell that much, but I can't read what it says. I forward it to Rachel.

It takes her a while. Then her email translation comes through.

It is our policy not to reveal the private address of artists. We will however be pleased to forward your request of interest to the artist concerned who may contact you directly.

I think that's right, Rachel has typed underneath. *More or less, anyway. Result! One step closer! You might be getting an email from your real mother any time now!!!!! Only she won't know it's you, will she? Just a student.*

We move from email to MSN messaging.

– Hmm, I type. Don't you think she just might recognise my name???? 'Emilywoodman' might jog her memory. Or do you reckon she is so off the planet she won't even notice that????

– *The reality is,* Rachel types back to me, *she has probably been WAITING FOR THIS MOMENT for years.*

– So why hasn't she contacted me???

– *Because she feels bad, perhaps. And because she*

wants YOU to seek her out, for it to be YOUR CHOICE, of course.

– I'm scared.

– *So? You're not going to let that stop you now!!*

– No.

– *Anyway, it might take some time before the gallery sends on your message, so forget about it for now if you can.*

– I'll try.

– *Come to the pavilion with me on Friday night. Luke's band is playing.*

– I might.

– *You could bring Seb.*

– Maybe.

– *Which means no. Are you ashamed of us or what? We are your friends!! How come you won't let us meet him?*

– I don't know. I will. Just not yet.

Friday, I'm home early. Cassy and Dad won't be back until at least six, four hours away. I turn on my laptop as usual, flick the kettle switch, plonk a tea bag in a mug. I prop the caravan door open to let in some fresh air. I settle myself down with my mug of tea in the shaft of sunlight that falls through the open door, laptop on my knees.

I open my emails.

You may not know this sender. Mark as safe . . .

The first new message in my inbox: *frandavids*

Hand shaking, I click on it.

My eyes are blurry to begin with, my heart fluttering.

I make myself breathe slowly, in, out, so I can take in the words.

Dear Emily

Your message was forwarded to me by the Musée d'art moderne. Thank you for getting in contact. I would be delighted to send you more information about my work for your photography project if you send me your postal address. Recently I've been painting more than taking photographs, but I will help if I can. What is your project about?

With best wishes

Fran

The language is strangely formal. I read the email over again, looking for signs she's guessed it's me, or for some veiled message hidden in the words, but I can't find anything.

Has she really not understood who I am?

Or is she trying to keep her distance?

And yet she didn't have to write back at all, did she?

I'm still poring over it when Seb turns up. He reads it with me.

'She's being cautious,' Seb suggests. 'Wanting to be really sure it is you. There might be someone else with the same name. That's why she wants your address. What have you said back?'

'Nothing, yet.'

He stretches out his legs and waits for me to type. My hands are trembling.

Dear Fran

I'm very happy to hear from you. I'm living in a caravan at the moment while Dad does up the new house, so please send anything you can c/o my friend Seb.

'You don't mind, do you?' I ask him. 'That way there's less chance of Dad and Cassy finding out.'

''Course,' Seb says.

I think hard what else to say.

My project is about trees, and my emotional connection to them. I like the paintings Emily Carr does of trees and they have influenced my work; so have the photos by Ansel Adams and Charlie Waite. Thank you for any help you can give me.

Emily Anna Woodman

Enough clues there, surely?

I press *Send*.

'Good,' Seb says. 'Now come for a run with me. You need to do something physical.'

If Seb were running at his usual pace there's no way I'd keep up, but he's not. He's being kind to me. After a while my feet find a kind of rhythm, and my breathing steadies. We start by going up the lane, turn right for a mile or so, then across the fields to a footpath that runs along the riverbank. It's much easier here, on the level.

'You're not bad,' Seb says, 'for a beginner.'

'Don't patronise me!' I try to thump him, but he's sprinting ahead, always just out of reach, and soon I'm out of breath.

He waits for me to catch up, but then he's off again. 'Come on. Push yourself! It's all in the mind, running.'

We run past Moat House, on the other side of the river. Three vans are parked up outside on the muddy field, and the sound of drilling and hammering echoes over the water. It's odd, seeing it all from this side of the river, more objectively: just a beautiful old house being tastefully restored.

'I still can't imagine living there,' I say to Seb.

'Why not? It'll only be a few months now,' he says.

'I know, but I can't imagine it. I can't see myself there.'

Seb slows right down. 'I don't know what you mean.'

'It's hard to explain,' I say. 'It's like I have to see myself somewhere, to make it happen. Visualise it. And with Moat House, I can't. Not any more.'

Seb frowns slightly. 'But it looks good,' he says. 'The stonework is all done. It's just the superficial stuff left to do now.'

I'm panting and so hot I feel sick. 'Can we stop for a bit?' I ask.

We walk for a few minutes, then Seb wants me to try again. 'One more mile, as far as the next bridge, then we'll turn back.'

'I'm so thirsty! And I'm getting a stitch.'

'You look lovely,' Seb says, 'all sweaty and pink.'

'Yeah, right.' I stick out my tongue.

Seb grabs me, pulls me in close. We kiss. We're both slippery with sweat.

'Back to the caravan, then? Walk a bit, run a bit. It's less than three miles.'

He doesn't mind me being useless at running. 'There's no rush,' he says, when we're almost home. 'It's not about that. It's like anything: you get better with practice.'

It does feel good, as soon as we stop. I'm glowing and full of energy, not tired out like I expected. I gulp down a glass of water.

'I need a shower,' I say.

'Me too.'

'I'll see if I can find you a towel,' I say. 'We don't have spares of things because there's no space.'

'I can share yours,' he says.

I pull a face. 'I don't think so!'

We've only been out about an hour, so Cassy and Dad won't be back for ages, which is just as well. I know Dad wouldn't want me going to the shower with Seb. But I pick up the shampoo, anyway, and find two clean towels and some coins for the meter, and we cross the field together to the concrete shower block.

'I can't believe you've had to do this all winter,' Seb

says. 'You must be tougher than you look.'

'Tough as old boots,' I say, and he laughs.

We take it in turns to shower. I go first. It's a bit strange, stripping off in the cubicle, with him just the other side of the door. I turn the shower on full blast, so it heats up quickly before I get under. I spend ages, turning slowly round in the hot water, letting it drum on my scalp, my back, my legs. I let the water stream over my face, hot and delicious. For a second, I let myself imagine what it would be like with Seb in the shower with me. I imagine his face, close up and wet, and our mouths together.

'Hurry up!' Seb calls. 'You're taking ages!'

When I open the door, he's there, grinning at me, already stripped to the waist. 'Your turn!' I say.

I think about him while I'm drying my hair under the wall heater. There's something so . . . so *intimate*, about doing all this together: the run, the shower . . .

He comes out after only a few minutes, his hair dripping, feet bare, teeth chattering. 'You took all the hot water!'

'Seb! I'm so sorry! You should've said. I'd have put in more coins.'

'It's OK. Come here, you.' He takes the towel and rubs my hair dry for me at the back, and then he kisses my bare neck, and along my collarbone.

'You're not actually tough at all, are you?' Seb says, running his finger along the curve of my neck to the top of my spine. 'Tender as the night.'

I laugh. 'Is that a book or a film?'

'Both. Except that I think it's *is* rather than *as* the

night.' He pulls me round and holds my damp face between his hands, and kisses me on the lips.

I pull gently away. I know he wants more from me, but I'm still not ready. Not yet. 'Come on, then,' I say. 'It's too cold to stay here much longer.'

We go back to the caravan together. We don't say much as we cross the field. Our hands hold tight.

Inside, I hang the wet towels over the rail and switch on the heater to warm the place up. 'Can you stay for supper?'

Seb nods.

'I'll start cooking, ready for when Dad and Cassy get back.'

'Will they mind me being here?'

'No. Cassy really likes you.'

'And your dad?'

'Him too. He's just a bit . . . odd about stuff. Protective, I suppose. Don't say anything about the shower.'

Seb watches me fill the pan with water, start chopping the garlic and onion. 'What shall I do?'

'Grate the cheese? Clear the table? There's not much to do.'

It's cosy, making supper together in the caravan, just us. I could live like this, I think. In a caravan, in a field somewhere, just me and Seb. I can see that. I can imagine it really easily.

11

I have to wait two whole weeks, and then just when I've almost given up, Seb sends me a text.

Your parcel's just arrived. Shall I bring it over later? xxx

Yes please! xxx I text him back.

I think about it all through English. Do I really want to open a parcel from Francesca in the caravan? With Cassy and Dad around?

I text him again at lunchtime.

Can you borrow the car? Can we go somewhere instead, after school?

Can't get car till later tonight. Mum's at work. 8? Come back to my place.

The day drags.

I had this fantasy of Seb and me going to our special place in the wood, and me opening the parcel there. But it will be too dark, and it's silly, really.

He picks me up at the top of the lane. I'm twitchy with nerves.

'Good day at school?' Seb asks.

'Not really. What did you do?'

'Not a lot. Read the stuff they sent for the Level Two course.'

It's hard for me to focus properly on what he's saying.

'How big's the parcel?' I say.

'Not very.' He glances at me, then back on to the road. 'Like, the size of a book. A thin one.'

I'm already preparing to be disappointed, shutting down something deep inside me that had just begun to open and breathe again.

He pulls up at his house.

'Is your mum in?' I don't feel like seeing anyone, not yet. And Avril asks too many questions.

'She won't bother us if I ask her not to. She's got a friend coming round, anyway. And Dad's out.'

The parcel is waiting for me on his bed. My name is written in thick blue pen on the front, with Seb's name and address underneath. I know the writing. It's just the same as on the albums, only bigger and fatter because of the felt-tip pen. She's tied it round with blue string. Her address is written on the back. I stare at the words. *Pyrénées-Atlantiques*.

The search is over, then. I have the address right here, in front of me. And the parcel? I'm almost too scared to open it.

Seb goes downstairs. I know he's thought about this, that he's giving me some space.

I sit on his bed, and turn the parcel round, and over, and then I start to unpick the knot in the blue string, and unpeel the sticky tape, and rip the layers of brown paper, and finally the contents lie there in my hands.

A thin booklet, the brochure from an exhibition. An envelope with a cardboard back, with photographs inside. I shake them out on to the bed: trees, and more trees. Fir trees, and trees with moss and lichen dripping from the branches, and the bare roots of a huge tree pulled out of the earth.

I'm numb.

I turn over the pages of the booklet. The writing is in French. There are photos of three paintings by Fran Davidson. The biggest one shows a young woman at a round table with a blue bowl of red cherries in the middle; behind her, two small children are sort of floating, as if they are almost sitting at the table but not quite. An open window. A fine muslin curtain blowing out, as if in a summer breeze. Outside, through the open window, a garden with an orchard of cherry trees.

Seb comes back upstairs with two cups of tea. He sits beside me on the bed. He looks at the painting. He looks at my face. 'Ghost children,' he says, eventually.

'Me and Kat.'

Seb pinches my arm. 'Except you're not. Not a ghost.'

'No.'

I feel dazed, as if I'm sleepwalking, going through the motions of something, not really there.

'Is there a letter?' Seb asks.

'I don't know.'

'Shall I see?'

I nod. He picks up the big brown envelope, fishes

209

out a smaller blue envelope, hands it to me. The paper is thin, flimsy.

'Shall I stay or go?' Seb asks.

'Stay. Please.'

I have to read it three times, very slowly.

Dearest Emily,

You cannot imagine how many times I have gone over this moment in my mind. Hoping it might happen, one day. When I got your email it was as if my heart stopped still. I can hardly believe it is happening, and that you have managed to find me – more importantly, that you have wanted to do so.

You must be sixteen now, old enough to know what you are doing. Old enough to understand some difficult things. But how do I begin to tell you? Little by little, perhaps.

I am so thrilled that you are studying photography. I would love to see your photos. Do send me some. Please?

Does your father know you have made contact with me? I wrote to him about three years ago but I never heard back. And Katharine? How is she?

I imagine you have many questions. Well, we have made a beginning, you and I. Write to me again, Emily. Send me something of you. Please.

With love

Fran

Seb reads it too. He holds me tight, while I cry and cry, for the mother I can't remember.

'It's weird, though,' Seb says when I finally stop. 'Those tree photos she sent you. How similar they are to the ones you've done. Don't you think?'

I can't bear to leave all the stuff at Seb's house, after all. I put it back in the paper packaging, the string and envelope and everything, and Seb finds me a plastic bag to keep it all safely together, and I take it back to the caravan with me.

Cassy knows I've been crying. She doesn't ask why. She and Dad are already getting ready for bed.

I tuck the bag next to me, under the duvet, next to the stone mouse who nestles up against the window, at the edge of my bed. All night, I sleep with her things close to me, my hand on the thin blue paper.

I wake up early: I'm already making plans.

Notebook 3

Summer, Pyrénées-Atlantiques

1

We are almost there, after hours of travelling.

Bus, train, another train, and this last bus, now trundling off again, the engine struggling as it climbs the long slow hill towards Pau, in the French Pyrenees. Seb and I look at each other and grin. It's been hours and hours. The sound of the bus fades into silence. It's just us, now, in the middle of nowhere.

Except that it isn't, of course. Even here, in the foothills of the mountains, there are farms and houses and whole villages, tucked away out of sight. It seems a miracle that we've found our way this far: the junction of the lane and the main road, the signpost to the church and the village. *Her* village. Just like the map shows.

Seb shifts his backpack on to both shoulders, I pick mine up too, all dusty from the road, and we begin the walk down the lane. It winds between small hayfields, down a long, green valley between densely wooded hills. Behind us the mountains go up into cloud, so high you can't see the top.

We walk in silence, all talked out. The air is a relief after the long, hot bus ride: no air-conditioning, seats packed together. The small fields, the greenness, is another surprise after the long hours we spent on the train, speeding through a dry golden landscape of huge sunflower fields and maize and then miles and miles of pine forest, all baking in the sun.

Here, swallows loop low over the grass, snatching flies out of the air. It must be early evening, but I've lost track of time. The lane crosses a stream, but when we look down over the bridge the stream has dried to a muddy trickle. The light changes. Dappled sunlight falls through overhanging beech trees. We reach the first houses at the edge of the village: two big stone houses, and then a modern one with a gravel drive and a new car parked outside.

The lane turns a bend and we find ourselves in front of a church, in a large deserted paved square. Tubs of scarlet geraniums, a stone bench, a huge old tree throwing deep shadow. The church bell strikes six at exactly the moment we arrive, as if it's announcing we are here. But there's no one to see.

'I'll get out the map again,' I say.

We sit on the stone bench and I smooth out the crumpled paper for the hundredth time.

'Up past the church, and along a bit.'

The lane goes steeply uphill and then levels out. Almost immediately, I see the house. I know it from the photo: the way it stands at a right angle to the lane, the stone-tiled roof, the wood stacked up under the eaves. A wooden verandah runs along the front. Huge shuttered windows have been flung wide open to let in the evening sun. *She'll have done that . . .*

216

It's all so solid and real it's a shock. I've stared at this house so many times, in a flimsy creased photograph. I've imagined arriving here.

We've stopped still. I glance at Seb. He's tired, and dusty, and crumpled-looking. He's come all this way because I asked him. It's the longest time we've been completely alone together.

Voices from somewhere behind the house drift across the hedge. A woman and a man, in conversation, though we can't hear the words.

In a minute, I'll see her.

I make myself open the gate. The click of the latch sounds ridiculously loud. Seb's hand is on my back, a gentle pressure.

'You're holding your breath!' His mouth is warm at my ear. 'Breathe, Em!'

Before, and after. Like a hinge. This is the me before . . .

Suddenly, before I'm properly ready, prepared, she's standing right there in front of me. A dark-haired woman, with a smooth, tanned face, white shirt, blue trousers, flip-flops . . .

She says a word – not English, I don't catch it – and one hand flies to her mouth, as if to stop herself crying out. An expression I can't read – panic? fear? – floods her face. 'Emily?' Her voice is hesitant.

I can't speak. I go hot. I swallow hard, so I don't throw up.

What does she see? A girl with short dark hair, slim, anxious? A complete stranger . . .

She doesn't recognise me.

217

And why would she? I was a toddler the last time. Not much more than a baby, with a round face and dark hair that curled, wispy. Here, now, face to face with my mother for the first time since I was two, all I can do is stare.

She stares back. Slowly, she drops her gaze as if it's too uncomfortable. As if she is ashamed.

And something flares up in me, a white-hot rage, as if I am still only two years old and she has only just abandoned me. It is as simple and raw and overwhelming as that.

That image has become frozen in time, itself like a photograph. My mother, framed against the green and gold of hayfields in high summer, mountains behind, an edge of stone house to one side, the half-smile fading on her face.

2

Seb reaches out for my hand. He holds it tight, and the feel of him there, steady beside me, keeps me from turning and running, while Francesca babbles a kind of welcome, in her too-bright voice.

'Come on in! You must be exhausted! It's been hot today – I'll fetch us all a drink. Come on through.'

We follow her through the massive front porch into a dark, open-plan sitting room which goes up and up, two storeys high.

'Sit down,' she says. 'Make yourselves at home.' She waves towards the big sofa, as if we should sit there, while she goes deeper into the old house to get the drinks.

We stay standing. We're both much too sweaty and dusty from the journey to plonk ourselves down on the cream sofa with its plumped-up red and gold cushions. We're both suddenly shy.

'It smells really old,' Seb whispers.

I stare at the paintings in dark wooden frames hung on each wall: abstracts in the same flame colours as the cushions. Are they *hers*?

The air is musty with old woodsmoke and candle

wax and a lemony scent that might be furniture polish or possibly real lemons, because Francesca reappears at that moment with a tray of glasses and a jug of home-made lemonade and a bottle of some orange-coloured liqueur.

She looks surprised to see us standing there, awkwardly. 'We can go out into the garden,' she says, 'if you'd prefer?'

Her voice sounds foreign. Perfectly good English, but with an accent. Has that happened over the years she's been living in France? Or has she always sounded like that? It's another shock, to find that I don't know these simplest of facts. That I don't remember, and no one has said. That no echo of her voice has stayed inside me.

'Yes, outside. Thanks,' Seb says. He nudges me, embarrassed by my silence.

I'm still too churned up to speak.

A dark-haired man with a beard is sitting at a large wooden table in the garden, hidden from the lane. He must have been here all the time; it was his voice we heard, before. He stands up. 'Josep,' he says, holding out his hand. 'Welcome.' But he doesn't smile.

Seb and he shake hands; I sit down on one of the wooden chairs.

Francesca puts the tray on the table and passes round the drinks. She sits down next to Josep; he takes her hand.

I stare at the two hands, resting loosely on the table together. She speaks to him in a language I cannot understand: not French, nor anything I recognise even one word of. 'Eskuara,' she explains to me and Seb. 'The language of the Pays Basque.'

'So, how was the journey?' Francesca fiddles with her glass, moves the tray a little.

I'm still searching for something – anything – that might pull up some memory from when I was tiny.

Seb tells her about the trains, and the buses, and all of that. She pours us each a little glass of the spirit that flames and burns as it goes down my throat.

'You can fly to Pau,' Francesca says. 'Or Nice. That makes it easier.'

'We did it the cheapest way,' Seb says. 'And it was fun.'

Francesca flushes slightly. 'I'd have paid, if you'd asked, Emily.'

There's a long, difficult silence. I swallow down the rest of the orange liquid in my glass; it stings all the way down.

Francesca tries again. 'How long have you two been friends?'

Seb looks at me. 'Since October?'

I could say exactly how long: nine months, twenty-one days, if I wanted to. But I don't.

Francesca tops up the glasses. The fiery liquid begins to thaw me out. Josep starts to talk in English to me and Seb; to Francesca he talks only Eskuara. 'You have brought the sun, ' he says, and smiles. 'The weather here is like England. It rains much. Which is why it is so green. But for a few days more we will have sun, I think. We are very lucky!'

We watch the sun, low in the sky now, about to slip behind the mountain. The clouds have cleared from the tops. Shadows lengthen across the grass.

'I'll finish preparing the meal,' Francesca says. 'It won't be long. You two can wash, or rest, or do whatever you want. There is no rush here. That is the best thing of all.' She smiles at me, but with a hurt sort of smile.

We still haven't touched. I've hardly said a word to her. But then, what does she expect? Whose fault is that?

Josep shows us the way to the bedrooms up the big oak staircase. The rooms on the first floor lead off a kind of balcony with banisters, open to the huge living room below and you can look right down on to the sofa and chairs and table we first saw when we arrived.

Josep opens one door after another. 'You can choose,' he says. 'This one here, or this.' He opens another door. 'One each, or one together, it is up to you. With a view of the mountain, or quiet at the front.' He laughs. 'It is all quiet.'

He goes downstairs again, to let us decide.

Seb and I go into each. It's easy to choose. Seb closes the heavy door and pushes me playfully on to the big bed with its thick blue quilt. He presses his face up close to mine. 'Hey,' he says, 'how cool is this!'

My body begins to melt beneath his. But my mind is still whirling. I slide out from under him, sit up.

222

'She doesn't like me,' I say. 'I can tell she doesn't like us being here.'

'That's ridiculous!' Seb says. 'It's hard for her, that's all. It's the same for her as it is for you, Em. Relax a bit. Stop punishing her. Stop being so cross.' He puts his arms back round me, and I let myself lean into him. I'm tired to the bone.

The smell of garlic and woodsmoke drifts up from the kitchen. A chair scrapes across a stone floor.

'We'd better go down.' I take his hand and trace the lines on his palm with my finger: the long life-line, right round under his thumb. I let it go again.

'Not yet.' Seb kisses me. 'There's no rush, she said. Wait a bit. Have a rest, then the meal together will go better. Lie down with me for a little while.'

We lie together on the top of the quilt. I close my eyes, but even though I'm so tired, my mind's too busy to let me sleep. I listen to Seb's breath: in, out, slow and steady as a purring cat. I open my eyes and watch his lovely, familiar face; the way his dark hair flops over, his dark eyebrows and lashes, the stubble round his chin and neck. The rise and fall of his chest. He sleeps for ages, innocent as a baby, and I lie and watch him, while the light outside fades and the room fills with shadows.

'Supper's ready!' Francesca calls up the stairs. 'Come on down.'

'Seb?'

He opens an eye. 'What?'

'Supper time.'

223

He yawns and stretches. 'Did you sleep?'

'A bit, I think. Dozed.'

We smooth the creases from our clothes. 'We haven't even washed!' I say.

We rinse our hands and faces quickly in the little bathroom at the end of the balcony. We leave grubby marks on the white towels.

Seb shrugs. 'It doesn't matter,' he says. 'She won't mind.'

Francesca has changed out of her linen trousers into a green silk dress. She's pinned up her hair in a loose sort of bun. As she dishes out portions of meat and vegetables from a large enamel pan, I watch the way she frowns, concentrating. I do that.

Her face looks thinner with her hair up, more angular in the light from the candles that Josep brings to the table from a dark wooden cupboard. Behind her, on a whitewashed wall, hangs a huge oil painting of a woman doing almost exactly what Francesca is doing this moment: serving food at a table, only the woman in the painting is large and rounded and wearing an apron round her middle, and there are children sitting at the table – two small girls.

The ghost children.

Josep sees where I'm looking. 'An early Fran Davidson,' he says. 'You like it?'

Francesca barely pauses, but she does, enough for me to know she's listening.

'Yes,' I say. 'It's like the one in the catalogue, from that exhibition.'

'Part of a series,' Josep says. 'Mothers and children.'

Francesca drops the serving spoon, and it clatters on to the table. She wipes her face with the back of her hand, goes out to the kitchen to get a cloth to wipe up the spilled food.

My face burns. *She can paint mothers, but not be one.*

Seb squeezes my hand. I know he's willing me not to speak, not to mess things up right now.

Francesca takes her place at the table. She holds her hands out, as if she's about to say grace, like a blessing in church, but she doesn't say anything. Josep pours us all wine, even though neither Seb nor I like it much. He starts to tell Seb about the problems with the rural economy, second homes in the Pays Basque, local young people having to leave the land. Francesca joins in from time to time, helping to explain things, or to translate a word.

I stop listening. I'm noticing how everything in this house looks as if it has been arranged, placed there like objects in a still-life painting. A bowl of peaches on a dark wooden chest; the cream candles on the table, the candlelight winking off the silver cutlery and throwing shadows. Perhaps that's what you would do if you were an artist. It would matter to you, how things looked.

I push my plate back. I'm too tired to eat anything. All I want to do is sleep.

'How is Kat?'

The directness of Francesca's question throws me completely off guard. I just answer it, without thinking. 'She's fine,' I say. 'She enjoyed her first year at uni. She's travelling this summer with her boyfriend, Dan. Cambodia and Laos.'

Francesca's eyes look shiny in the candlelight. She pours herself another glass of wine. 'Did you – have you brought photographs, to show me? Of her, and you, and your dad?'

Josep stops talking for a second, then he turns back to Seb.

'A few,' I say. 'Mostly I brought photos from my project.'

I don't tell her how furious Kat is about me coming here, to see Francesca. How she wants nothing to do with her: *Not EVER!*

'I'm so pleased you are here, Emmy.' Francesca's voice is so quiet I have to lean forward to hear her. Two red spots flame on her cheeks.

Emmy. The word sings in my head.

Josep clears the dishes, and brings out a glass bowl of fruit salad and a plate of almond cakes. He makes coffee.

I can hardly keep my head up.

Finally the meal is over. 'You go and get some sleep,' Francesca says. 'We can talk and look at photographs tomorrow. Which room have you chosen?'

'The blue one,' Seb says.

'You will wake up to the view of the mountains.'

I push back my chair. 'Thanks for the meal and everything,' I say.

'Sleep well. See you in the morning. As late as you want.'

* * *

Seb follows right behind, helping me up the wooden stairs. Neither of us is used to eating so late, or to drinking red wine, or brandy or whatever it was in the little glasses. We giggle softly: too much wine, too much everything.

I wash in the bathroom; by the time Seb comes back to the room I'm already in bed, flopped out against the pillows. 'It's so soft! Everything's so squishy and luxurious and comfortable! And I'm *sooo* tired.'

Seb tugs his T-shirt over his head, steps out of his jeans, climbs next to me on the bed. He strokes my face very gently. 'You're exhausted. It's not surprising. That journey, meeting your mother for the first time . . .'

'Not the first time,' I start to say, although sleep is already creeping through my body, slurring my speech. Just before I let myself go completely, I hear Seb whisper very softly in my ear.

'I love you, Emily Anna Woodman. Know that?'

3

Love. The word turns me over. Especially in Seb's soft, deep voice.

I wake up to find him already out of bed, tugging on shorts. 'Going for a run,' he says. 'Won't be more than a hour.'

He closes the bedroom door behind him. I drift in and out of sleep. The sun gets higher; it creeps into one corner of the room, lighting the wall into a brighter blue, glancing off the brass handles on the chest of drawers and the mirror glass. The beam of sunlight strengthens and broadens.

When I next surface from sleep, the sun is shining directly on the little painting on one wall: the only one in this room, and on a very different scale to the rest of the artwork hanging elsewhere in the house. The small square seems to come more sharply into focus in the sunlight, so that I notice it properly for the first time. The painting shows three trees, though more an abstract idea of trees than real ones. The dense, dark green around them suggests a bigger, dark green forest surrounding these three. As the sun shifts across the room, it lights up the smallest tree in the

centre so that it glows, a vibrant emerald, as if it's
alive, a flame almost. It's as if I can see the spirit of
the tree, or its heart. It's hard to explain, but I feel a
sudden deep connection with it. I love this little painting. It seems familiar, as if I've seen it somewhere
before: a postcard of it, or a picture in a book,
perhaps? Because how can I have seen it for real,
when it's hanging here, on a bedroom wall, in a
Pyrenean farmhouse?

I lie in the bed, half awake, half dreaming, and suddenly filled with happiness. It's the little tree,
working a kind of magic on me. A tingle of excitement
dances up and down my spine.

My mother is someone extraordinary.

Yesterday's anger has been washed away by my
night of deep rest, wrapped round by Seb's tenderness. Today, anything might happen.

The house is silent. Outside, birds are singing their
hearts out, the way they do in the early morning
before the day heats up. The strip of sun gets wider,
until the whole room is flooded with it. I drift back
into sleep, and out again, hardly knowing which is
which. The painting glows. The trees look as if they
are moving, swaying in the breeze that stirs the
muslin at the window. I can smell their deep resinous
pine branches. The air hums with insects. Under my
feet the old pine needles are thick and soft. Sunlight
slants between rows of trees and makes patterns:
dark, light, dark, light – zebra stripes. I'm walking in
the forest between the trees. It's getting lighter, as if
we're almost at the edge, where the trees are spaced

out and grass and moss grows in thick patches. There are two of us, walking together, getting closer . . .

I open my eyes. I'm back in the blue room. Nothing has changed but the light, and the sounds. Voices from downstairs, a door creaking open, feet tapping across a hard floor. Laughter.

I slide off the bed and go to the window. The mountains look sharp in the morning light: it brings them closer. Everything has come into focus; between the hills and the garden are the series of small fields we walked through to get here, yesterday. In the nearest field just beyond the garden a man in blue overalls is cutting the clover by hand with a scythe, a small dog leaping and running along the swathe of cut clover he leaves in his wake. It's like a scene in a film, and so strange to see it for real, just outside the window. I almost go and fetch my camera, still unpacked in my bag. The colours are good: the bright green clover, the blue overalls, the black and white dog.

Josep walks across the garden. I draw back so he doesn't see me at the window. I hear a car engine start up, and not long after, I see a car going along the lane through the fields to the main road.

I get dressed quickly. Not the hot black jeans and creased T-shirt, but a thin cotton skirt, and a sleeveless top, and flip-flops. I run my fingers through my hair, splash my face with cold water, brush my teeth. I go downstairs quickly, before Seb or Josep get back. It seems very important that it's just Francesca and me, alone in the house.

I can't find her at first. She's not in the kitchen or

the living room. I think of calling out her name – but *Francesca* sounds wrong, and I can't yet bring myself to call her Fran.

I help myself to a peach from the bowl, and take it outside to eat at the garden table. And there she is: pouring coffee into a blue china cup, talking to a small tortoiseshell cat.

Francesca looks up. 'This is Marthe,' she says. The cat weaves round her legs, rubbing its head against her cupped hand. 'Sometimes she lives in the house, sometimes not. She goes off to have her kittens. She doesn't like to have them in the house.'

'She's not much more than a kitten herself.'

'No. But she's two, nearly three. Three litters already, and she must have another lot: she's got milk, see? She's feeding them.'

Francesca pours milk from the jug on the table into her saucer and puts that on the grass. We watch the cat lapping furiously, purring at the same time; her whole body quivers with delight.

'I saw Seb on his way out,' Francesca says. 'You slept well? I thought you'd be later than this. At your age I'd sleep until midday!'

At my age. Francesca, at seventeen. I try to imagine her. One year before she met Dad.

'The sun woke me up.'

'You can close the shutters, if you like. It'll get hot in there. We close the shutters to keep the house cool when we get a hot spell, like now. In the winter, the shutters keep the warmth in. It gets miserably cold.'

She's talking about the weather, and time is ticking

231

away. Any moment, and Seb will come back!

'Coffee?'

I shake my head. 'Let's talk. Properly.'

She goes still.

I plunge in. 'It's weird. I thought about meeting you such a lot. But it isn't like I imagined. It's a shock, that we don't know each other at all. I thought I might see you and memories would flood back, but I don't remember a thing. If I'd passed you in the street I'd never have known it was you.'

Francesca frowns. She sips the coffee from the blue cup cradled in both hands.

I keep talking. 'I want you to explain it to me. Why you went. How you could do that. I want to hear what you say.'

She swallows hard, puts down the cup. The cat mews for more milk, and when Francesca doesn't immediately oblige, jumps right up on the table.

'Off! Shoo!' She shoves the cat hard. It stares back at her, indignant, and stalks off.

'It's unthinkable, isn't it? Looking at you now . . . I know it was crazy and terrible. The act of a mad woman.'

She doesn't look mad.

'I'll have to tell you the whole story,' she says at last. 'It will take a while. And maybe you still won't understand, or forgive me.'

It's as if I'm the one in charge, I think then. I feel as if I'm older than her, like I do with Cassy some-times. Francesca looks crumpled and defeated, not the *breathtakingly selfish woman* who gave us up,

232

according to Dad and Kat.

'But you've turned out so well, without me . . . perhaps it was the right thing to do, after all . . .'

I can't believe she said that. As if it could ever be *right*, what she did. It leaves me numb. I turn away.

She knows she's made a mistake, saying those words. When I finally look at her again, I see tears in her eyes.

Crying isn't going to help, I nearly say. *What right have you got to cry?*

But I can hear Seb's voice in my head, softly persuasive. *You've come so far. Em. It's hard for her too. Anyone can see that.* Seb, with his generous heart, talking to me in the dark.

'Go on, then,' I say instead. 'Tell me.'

4

'It starts – where? Your dad and me, I suppose, meeting when I was in my first year of art school in London, and he was doing his architecture degree: first part of a long training. We moved in together. I got pregnant: unexpectedly, too soon in our relationship, really, though we were pleased too. We loved each other. We were happy, as well as scared. And broke. That was Katharine.

'But it was hard for me, still trying to study and carry on with all that, at the same time as being pregnant and getting bigger. I didn't have so much energy, suddenly. Didn't want to go out all the time – not with my arty friends or Rob's architect ones, either. Drinking, staying up all night – you can't do that when you're eight, nine months pregnant. Not with a new baby, either.

'She was born in the summer. That was good. It was college holidays. We spent some time with my mother: she'd come over and rented a house for us all in Wales. It was her chance to see her first grandchild. At one point, she suggested we all go back with her to Canada. But it was a silly idea. Rob was doing his degree, his career just unfolding. And we didn't get on, my mother and I. A summer was just about OK, not any longer. We had big arguments. She was so critical of everything I did. I was a big disappointment to her, having a baby so young, not having a career.'

Francesca can see my impatience. 'It's all relevant,' she says. 'I have to tell it like this.

'I didn't finish art school. I couldn't, with baby Kat. It seemed sensible for Rob to carry on, with my support, because we knew that once he'd qualified as an architect he'd earn heaps more money than I ever would as an artist.'

'Not necessarily,' I say. 'Some artists make millions.'

'And most don't make a bean. You know that, Emily.'

'So, that's how it went on. Rob having to work really long hours. Kat growing up, me looking after her, still doing a little photography, but not much, and some painting, and keeping myself ticking over, creatively speaking. I'd make things for Kat, or me, or Rob: clothes, a quilt for the cot, things like that. We bought our own house, with help from the money my mother left me. She died around that time . . . and I was already pregnant with you by then.'

'Another mistake.'

'No, no – not planned, exactly, but it was fine. It meant we were a proper family. We thought it would be lovely for Kat – and it was. Rob was happy. We moved house again – he dreamt houses, even, then! He loved that house, further out in the countryside, with woods nearby, like he'd played in as a child. He thought that was what children needed: space, and a garden and all that. But things started going wrong for me.'

I can't bear to look at her. Her face, wet with tears, her hands holding her head as if the pain of talking about it is weighing her down.

'I was so lonely. Rob was away all day, working till late. I didn't have anyone close. I felt crushed. I hardly knew who I was, any more. I lost myself totally.'

I can guess the rest. I don't want to hear her spell it all out. She goes to an art class. She starts life drawing. Her teacher is this amazing, attentive man: dark-haired, olive-skinned, good-looking. Pierre encourages her. He tells her how talented she is. She feels alive again. Under his tender touch, she feels herself coming back to herself. And when it's time for him to go back to France, he asks her to go with him. And she does.

It's an agony to her, I can see that, to tell me what she did.

'I left you. It was a terrible thing to do. And more than that, I was a total coward. If I cut you out of my life completely, no contact at all, I could pretend not to feel anything. I would eventually stop imagining what it was like for you. But how can you pretend about such deep, important things for long? You would truly go mad, to keep that shut down inside. So it came out in paintings. Hundreds of paintings, most of them awful, too raw and ugly to show. And just a few that I kept, and eventually showed to other people, and they liked them, and I began a different life as an artist. And the passion with Pierre had burned out by then: fast, furious, as that kind of love is. Not lasting. But I had myself back by then. I would survive.'

She weeps, and I won't look at her, or touch her, or comfort her. She wants me to forgive her, even though she hasn't asked, not outright, and just as well, because the answer would be no.

5

Neither of us hear Josep's car returning. When I stand up, I see Josep outlined in the doorway, watching us, waiting for the right moment he can go to her, comfort her.

I make myself walk towards the gate, but as soon as I'm through to the lane, I start running. I don't have a clue where I'm going. I just need to escape, just keep moving: one foot, the other foot.

I try to remember what Seb says. Keep the breathing steady: in, out. It's all in the mind, running.

I follow the lane as it winds along the contours of the land, slightly uphill all the way, so I start getting out of breath, my heart hammering. It goes more steeply for a while and then peters out altogether, becoming a rough track. My sides are aching. I stop to take deep, racking breaths, and I start to cry. I walk, cry, walk up the winding track, up to where it finally stops, in a hay meadow that hasn't yet been mown. I walk through the long grass right to the middle of the field, and lie down, flat on my back. Above me bees and flies and biting insects hover and hum, and the grass seed rustles as the wind blows through it. The sky is a deepening blue, and the sun goes higher, and gets hotter and hotter, burning down and baking the earth. Finally I've no more tears left.

There, I think. That's done with. It's all over.

Not long after I've finished crying, I sit up. I don't know what makes me look – it's too far off for me to hear footsteps, yet – but from my viewpoint high in the hay meadow I spot a small figure hurrying along the lane in the valley, a tiny ant in the green landscape. She keeps going, up and up, until she disappears from sight.

And then she appears again, right at the edge of my field.

I don't move. I don't lie down, to hide. I wait to see what she does.

She's already seen me.

She walks slowly through the long grass, and she comes and sits on the grass right next to me. It's as if she's thought out what she's going to do, that she's made some sort of decision and won't let herself stop now.

She picks up my hand and holds it between both of hers. I let her. I don't pull away, or anything. Her hands feel cooler than mine.

We sit for ages, silent, in the middle of the field, like that.

I didn't expect her to come after me. Lying in the grass, I'd imagined the scene I left behind in the garden: Josep comforting her, making her more coffee. I imagined her climbing the stairs to the bathroom, swooshing cold water over her swollen, tear-stained face, wiping her hands on the white towel. I imagined her going back to sit with Josep in the sunny garden. I saw it all as vividly as if I was actually there.

But I was wrong about her.

She lets my hand go. She pulls her hair back from her face and over her shoulder in a gesture that is so like Kat I want to hug her and tell her so. One day, maybe I will.

She starts talking to me, her eyes very direct, and bright.

'Thank you for listening to all that. For letting me speak. I know it was horrible. Too hard for anyone to hear. And thank you for searching me out in the first place, and for coming all this way. It was a brave thing to do, Emmy. Brave and bold.'

I look at her. 'I couldn't have done it without Seb,' I say. 'It was Seb loving me like he does that made me brave.'

'Well, I'm glad for Seb, then,' Francesca says. 'But you are still courageous, Emily. My beautiful daughter. In spite of what I did to you.'

We talk some more as we walk back down to the house together.

'Really, I'm fine,' I say. 'I survived, didn't I? Dad did a good job. Dad and Cassy.'

'More than good,' Francesca says.

I tell her about their new baby. 'I'm looking forward to it, now,' I say, and I find it's actually true: I am! It's funny how things change.

* * *

I go upstairs for a shower. I lie on the blue quilt in the bedroom for a while, afterwards. Someone has closed the shutters, and the room is deliciously cool. Without the sunlight on it, the three trees in the painting look flat, now, instead of alive and glowing. I lie on the bed, and think about Francesca's story.

Was it worth it? I wonder. Giving up everything? Just so she can paint? I think of everything she has lost.

Seb stays out of my way all day. At some point in the late afternoon, I get up and have another shower, and when I go downstairs I find the three of them sitting in the garden. Josep brings out a tray of drinks. Francesca doesn't say much. She goes into the house to finish making our meal.

I'm exhausted, even though I have slept most of the afternoon. Seb comes up with me as soon as we have finished eating. We lie together side by side, and he smooths my hair back from my face, and he kisses me.

'I've wanted to do that all day,' he says to me.

His tenderness makes me cry all over again. How can there be so many tears?

The next morning, Francesca takes me to her studio, in one of the outhouses in the garden.

'I don't let many people in here,' she says.

It's messy, with piles of paper and frames stacked against the rough whitewashed walls. An old paint-splashed trestle table under the window is covered with pots of paint and brushes in jam jars and odd things like a piece of wood and a pile of stones and a load of books propped open with old, stained coffee cups. A plan chest like Dad's, with lots of thin drawers, stands at the other end of the barn, and there's a mat and a wooden chair with a faded blue cushion.

'You have the chair,' Francesca says. 'We'll look at your work first, yes?' She sits on the floor, at my feet. She pays each photograph proper attention. My heart's hammering; I'm nervous about what she'll say. Suddenly it matters to me, where it didn't, before.

'This one: I love this. The composition, the light; the way the shadow falls on his face. This one is good, Emmy.' She smiles. 'It takes a long time. You have to find your own style, something special that is just yours. You start by looking at what other artists do. Sometimes you copy; try the same things. But you must go on, push yourself further. Not everyone can do that. This picture is good because I feel the emotion behind it. The way you are looking at the boy.'

'Seb.'

She flips through the others again. She picks out the willows, and the avenue of sycamores and the beech tree with the sunset. 'Trees are special for you too,' she says. Her voice catches.

'That little painting in the blue bedroom –' I start to say.

'From a long time ago. One of the first I did, way back, as a student.'

'I love it,' I tell her. 'And it's like I know it already. Like I've seen it somewhere before.'

Fran hunches her knees up, hugs them to her. 'It

hung in the house,' she says. Her voice sounds strained, too tight in her throat. 'When you were a baby. But you can't possibly remember that. Can you?'

I shrug. Can I? Maybe it is possible.

'More likely it reminds you of something else,' Francesca says. 'It's a bit derivative. My Emily Carr phase! I hadn't found my own style, back then.'

'The man you went away with,' I say. 'The one you fell in love with. What happened to him? Why didn't it last?'

'I don't know . . . Maybe because of what I'd given up, for him? The stakes were too high. Who knows? Or perhaps because we didn't really know each other well enough. We rushed into it.

'I lived in his house to begin with. But the winter was cold and wet and horrible. Everything was hard work. I wasn't used to chopping wood to heat a house. I couldn't drive in those days. I was trapped in the house. The passion burned out. But I was painting all the time by then. Pierre helped me get that first important exhibition. He was good to me. I sold some work. I made a tiny bit of money for myself, but more importantly, I started to believe I could do this. And after a while I moved out, and rented a place by myself. That time alone was essential for me as an artist. I needed it, like people need air or food.

'Even when I met Josep, I knew I would still live alone. When I am in the middle of a painting I immerse myself completely. I don't want to do anything else or think about anyone else.' She looks at me sadly. 'How can you do that, as an artist, and be a mother too?'

'Some people manage it,' I say.

'Yes. But not me. And small children need so much of you. All of you, really. An adult might understand that: Josep does, though not all men would. Most would find it hard, perhaps. But a child – no. It is asking too much.'

I try to make sense of what she's explaining to me, but it hurts.

'You should have worked that out before you had children,' I say. 'It wasn't fair, what you did.'

'No.'

'Aren't you lonely? Living alone?'

'Yes. Of course. Though now I have lots of friends, and Josep stays here some of the time. But it's the life I have chosen. We each have to find our own way to live, and to love. Don't ever let anyone else tell you how it should be, for you.'

She stretches her legs out, and then she gets up. She touches her arm round my shoulders, briefly. 'Do you want to see some of my photographs, now?'

We open the drawers in the plan chest, and she shows me her photographs, and then the tree paintings, and finally we look together at the series of drawings for her mother-and-children paintings.

'The ghost children don't grow up, do they?' I say. 'They are all little. Like the age when you left us.'

Francesca can't speak. She's biting back tears again. She leans against the wall of the barn, her hand holding her head.

'It's all right,' I say to her. 'I think I understand it a bit, now. I'm glad you told me everything. It's better to know the truth about things.'

6

The river near here is called La Bidouze. Seb and I have been running along it each morning for the last five days, before it gets too hot, and today we saw two kingfishers flash across near the bridge, blue streaks of light.

Yesterday, we walked with Francesca and Josep to the top of the mountain we can see from the house: Pic de Belchou. *Walking into the view,* Josep calls it. All the way up, the air was full of the sound of bells, all different notes: the sheep as well as the cows wear thick leather collars with bells of different sizes depending on how old they are and their place in the herd. Josep explained how they still farm in the old ways here: in the spring, the animals are taken up from the farms into the hill pastures, where they stay for the summer. The bells guide the shepherds to their herds.

At the top of the mountain our mobiles actually got reception, unlike the house in the valley, and I read the two texts from Cassy and Dad:

Thinking of you. Missing you. Take care. Hope it's all going OK.

Hospital think baby will be here in next week or so. Moat House not ready!

We climbed back down a different way, through beech and sweet-chestnut woods. The trees have silver bark, and roots like fingers, and moss and lichens grow like long hair. 'It's a proper fairytale forest,' Francesca said. 'Like in a storybook.'

I told her about Kat and me, reading the storybook she left for us. I told her how we traced her name with our fingers, and about the picture I used to stare at, of the woman in the blue dress, leaning over the river, because I thought it was her.

Each day we are here, we are stitching something together, Francesca and I, Emily, her daughter. Piece by small piece. Filling in some of the gaps.

And at night, it's just Seb and me, laughing and talking in the dark. I've never been any place where it is quite so dark as it is here, on the hot, cloudy nights when there's no moon or stars.

We have three more days and nights like this. And then we'll travel back to our other lives: school and my AS results, and Cassy and Dad and the new baby, and Moat House, and Seb's new course at college. I'll have a whole new load of photographs to download.

Seb talks about working with stone, how it's like cutting a block of light: the line of the chisel makes the darkness and the shadow. As the shadow of each mark gets stronger, the light in the stone seems to get brighter. It's the opposite with a photograph: it's the light that you draw with, rather than the dark. But you still need the two: the dark and the light. You can't see one without the other. And I think the same is true with painting, and stories too.

When I was little, and Kat read me that fairy story about the woodcutter taking his two children into the forest and leaving them there, all I could think about was the children being abandoned and lost and afraid in the dark. What I realise now is that the story actually had a happy ending: the children came back. In spite of everything the adults did to them, the children found their own way home, their pockets full of precious stones and pearls that gleamed and shone in the light.

There's one last photograph I'm going to take before we leave. I've planned it out in my mind's eye. I'll rest the camera on the garden table, press the timer. The background will be the hayfield, and the mountain behind, going up into the clouds, and in the foreground my mother and I will be standing, side by side. I want to be able to remember how it has been here. I want to be able to hold the photo in my hand and see for myself the ways we are like each other, and the ways we are different. And then I'll be ready to go home. Seb and I together.

Acknowledgements

I'd like to thank Nicola Davies for one particularly helpful conversation we had; my son Jack for letting me borrow some of his Photography notes; my sister Sue for information about working with stone; the Creative Writing department at Bath Spa University for allocating me research time; and Emma and Diana, my editors at Bloomsbury.

About the Author

Julia Green is the Course Leader on the MA in Writing for Young People at Bath Spa University, and has had three novels published by Puffin and three by Bloomsbury: *Breathing Underwater*, *Drawing with Light* and *Bringing the Summer*. She lives in Bath.

Learn more about Julia and her writing with a brief Q & A.

When you were Emily's age, what kind of books did you like to read?

When I was Emily's age, I was reading books for A level English: *King Lear* and *Measure for Measure* by Shakespeare; contemporary plays like *The Royal Hunt of the Sun* by Peter Shaffer; novels by Thomas Hardy (*Tess of the d'Urbervilles*, *Far from the Madding Crowd*) and D.H. Lawrence (*Sons and Lovers*). I read *Wuthering Heights* by Emily Brontë, *Jane Eyre* by Charlotte Brontë, and *Pride and Prejudice* (Jane Austen). I started reading the Romantic poets about this time (Keats, Wordsworth) and also poetry by Dylan Thomas, Stevie Smith, Philip Larkin, Ted Hughes and Seamus Heaney. I loved Dodie Smith's *I Capture the Castle*; *Catcher in the Rye* (J.D. Salinger), and historical romances by Georgette Heyer and Jean Plaidy . . . I read widely, everything I could get my hands on! My parents loved books and our house was full of them. I had a brilliant English teacher called Miss Fox, and she suggested books to me too. We went to see a production of *The Tempest* by the RSC at Stratford-upon-Avon and I was blown away by how magical it was. I've never forgotten it. I use quotations from *The Tempest* in my novel *Breathing Underwater*.

When you are writing, to what extent do you draw on your own experiences?

All my stories are a mixture of 'real life', closely observed or remembered, and imagination. Different combinations of the real and the made-up. I do use my experiences a lot, but always re-imagined. Memories, thoughts and feelings are transformed in the writing of them. But that's not the same as saying my novels are autobiographical. They most definitely are not! My characters are not me. They are all imagined, created by me. But I need to feel a connection to the material I am writing.

How long does it take you to write a book?

Different novels take different amounts of time. I think and dream and imagine and write notes for a long while before I start writing down the story. Once I know enough to start typing on my laptop, it takes me about nine months to a year. *Breathing Underwater* took the longest: that's because I wrote one version then realised there was a better way to tell the story, with the parallel sections of 'This Summer' and 'Last Summer', and I rewrote the whole novel completely! I'm very proud of taking that time to get it right. I'm a slow writer because I think so much, and rewrite and edit a lot. Plus I'm not writing full-time: I have another job, as a university lecturer teaching Creative Writing.

What do you hope readers will take away from reading your books?

I hope my readers will immerse themselves in the story. I hope they will be able to 'see' the places I describe and imagine themselves there. I hope they will be moved and feel strong emotions alongside my characters, going on their own emotional journey. I hope they will think about things: their own lives, choices, friends, families, relationships. I hope they will put down the book at the end and feel satisfied and uplifted.

If you could recommend just one book for everyone to read, what would it be?

Impossible question, but if you could only read one book, it would have to be a children's book: *Tom's Midnight Garden* by Philippa Pearce. Like the best children's books, it's a book for readers of any age. It's a beautiful and moving story. It's perfectly constructed, I think, and profound about the connections between the young and the old, between past and present, and the importance of memory.

Why I wrote
Drawing with Light

I knew that I wanted my next novel to be a love story. Before I started, I wrote in my notebook *'I want to write about the transformative power of love: the way it changes you and opens you up to the world.'* I drew on some of my own memories of first love when I was creating the character of Seb. Gradually, I came to see that I was writing about lots of different kinds of love: the love between sisters, and the love between a man and a dog, love between friends, and the love that holds families together: not just parents and children, but step-parents too. Central to my story is the relationship between a mother and a daughter, and a big question: what could happen to make a mother abandon her own children? Could you ever forgive a mother who did that? This is the mystery at the heart of the novel.

While I was writing, the title I had in my head was 'Talking in the Dark', with all its associations with intimacy and secrets. It's what sisters do, and best friends, and lovers. I like the final title *Drawing with Light* because it's more uplifting and hopeful, which reflects the story more accurately, and because it is a reference to the art of photography, which is a very important strand in the story.

My favourite section in Drawing with light 🔦

I've chosen the first chapter in Notebook 3, Summer, Pyrénées-Atlantiques. It comes towards the end of the novel. The novel is divided into Emily's three notebooks: this helped me to structure the story and deal with the passage of time, and is also a 'nod' towards Dodie Smith's wonderful novel *I Capture the Castle*, in which her character Cassandra is writing in notebooks.

I've chosen this passage as it is the point where I first started writing the novel; it's where Emily finally meets her mother for the first time. I could 'see' the whole scene as if I was standing there watching it all unfold. I knew the place – I had been there a year or so before – and had a photograph of it on my desk: the mountains behind, the fields where hay-making was taking place. In my head I heard that first, hesitant encounter between Emily and her mother.

As I started to write, I began to see that the real story would be about what has brought Emily to this point, so that she feels strong enough to make such a difficult emotional journey. Falling in love, and being loved back by Seb, gives her that courage. I started to think about the mother's story. What has happened to her? How could she do such a terrible thing as abandon her own children? In the back of my mind were things I had read about women who have been artists as well as mothers (like the sculptor Barbara Hepworth, for example)

and for whom that has been an enormous tension and struggle. Maybe I was remembering what it was like for me when I was bringing up my small children and also wanting a creative life. I am fascinated by the whole question of how we can be good parents, and also not give up on our own deepest desires and needs.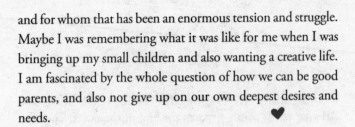

I had to imagine what it would feel like for both Francesca and Emily. I knew Emily would feel very angry, and I knew that anger is how people cover up hurt and sadness. I had to keep rewriting the scene to get the emotional feel of it 'right', as well as describing the setting where it's all unfolding.

After I'd first written this scene, I wrote in my notebook *'It's the end of the story . . . rather than the beginning!'*

Writing for me is a slow process of discovery: it seems as if the story already exists out there somewhere, and if I listen hard enough and pay sufficient attention, it will gradually come close enough for me to see exactly what it is.

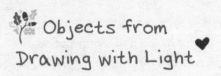 Objects from Drawing with Light

There are many layers of influence in this novel. There was my original journey to the house in the Pyrénées, and an earlier trip to the museum of modern art in Ceret, France.

While I was at a conference in Vancouver a few years before, I came across the amazing paintings of trees by Canadian artist Emily Carr. Earlier still, as a teenager, I loved Robert Frost's poems 'Birches' and 'Stopping by Woods on a Snowy Evening'; as a younger child I played in woods near my home and made a den under an oak tree with a friend.

By happy coincidence ('happenstance'), as I was beginning to write the novel, my younger son was beginning to learn about Photography for A level, and his exciting, experimental photographs were an inspiration to me for Emily's own photos. I borrowed some of his notes. Later, he took photographs of trees and rivers to help me further. My artist sister has a studio where she works on stone sculpture, and her work helped me develop that aspect of the story. I based the stone mouse that Seb makes for Emily on a replica of *Toby's* mouse from *The Children of Green Knowe* by Lucy Boston, which I bought at her ancient, beautiful house in Cambridgeshire when I visited it a few years ago. I keep the mouse on my writing desk . . .

Things to do after reading
Drawing with Light

★ Go to an art gallery. Look closely at the paintings you like or feel drawn to. Write about them in a notebook.

★ Find out about Emily Carr. One good book about her is *Beloved Land: The World of Emily Carr*, introduced by Robin Laurence (Douglas & McIntyre Ltd, Vancouver, 1996). Look online at www.emilycarr.ca for pictures that are in the Vancouver Art Gallery collection.

★ Take photographs. Look at work by Ansel Adams and Charlie Waite.

★ Go for a walk. Look closely at the trees! Sit under one to daydream, think and listen. Write a poem about the experience.

★ Read *I Capture the Castle* by Dodie Smith. It was written a long time ago, but it's a wonderful story and the central character is inspiring. Cassandra is seventeen and wants to be a writer . . .

★ Keep your own writing or photography notebook.

A room of my own

My attic is the place where I can escape to write. It is quiet at the top of the house, and from the skylight windows I can see hills and fields and trees and plenty of sky. It is full of books, some on shelves, others stacked high on the floor. There are piles of paper, boxes of old manuscripts, and photos, post-cards, other things that help me to write whatever story I am currently working on. It is very untidy but I know where everything is! A small carved mouse (Toby's mouse from *The Children of Green Knowe*) perches close to my laptop.

Fall in love with more breathtaking
stories from Julia Green

OUT NOW

www.julia-green.co.uk

JULIA GREEN

Bringing the Summer

OUT NOW

www.julia-green.co.uk